Born in Melbourne, Suzanne Hawley moved to Sydney and worked as an actor and then writer in television, film and theatre. She wrote the miniseries *Ring of Scorpio* (Nine Network) and received an AFI award as co-writer of *Bodysurfer* (ABC television). Suzanne received a Sydney Theatre Company award for her play *Concrete Palaces* and she is currently working as a writer and script editor on a new drama series for Network Seven.

Alison Says is Suzanne's first novel and, while she admits to teaching in secondary schools in Victoria, she insists this is NOT autobiographical.

Alison Says

SUZANNE HAWLEY

RANDOM HOUSE AUSTRALIA

Random House Australia Pty Ltd
20 Alfred Street, Milsons Point, NSW 2061
http://www.randomhouse.com.au

Sydney   New York   Toronto
London   Auckland   Johannesburg

First published by Random House Australia 2005
Copyright © Suzanne Hawley 2005

All rights reserved. No part of this publication may be reproduced, stored in a retrieval system, or transmitted in any form or by any means, electronic, mechanical, photocopying, recording or otherwise, without the prior written permission of the publisher.

National Library of Australia
Cataloguing-in-Publication Entry

Hawley, Suzanne.
Alison says.

ISBN 1 74051 348 7.

I. Title.

A823.3

Cover image by Robert Daly/Getty Images
Cover and internal design by Darian Causby/Highway 51 Design Works
Typeset in 12/14 Berkeley Book by Midland Typesetters, Maryborough, Victoria
Printed and bound by Griffin Press, Netley, South Australia

10 9 8 7 6 5 4 3 2

To my darling Jean-Pierre
for his joie de vivre.

Tuesday

Alison says I should write a diary. She's my shrink. 'Write anything,' she said, 'a stream of consciousness. It will become easier as you go,' she enthused. 'By actually writing things down it may help us shed light on what exactly is going on in your life. It will help us pinpoint those areas which are working . . . and those that are obviously not. And then we can begin remoulding and reshaping any destructive behaviour patterns and realigning them to a more productive way of life.

'And if you get stuck,' she added, 'if you can't think of anything to write, just write . . . "I can't think of anything to write".'

Wednesday

I can't think of anything to write.

Thursday

I can't think of anything to write.

Friday

It's raining outside. Cat from next door just threw up on the carpet.

Saturday

It's Saturday . . . all day . . . I can't think of anything to write.

Sunday

I have nothing to say.

Monday

Just as depressed as ever. This therapy is not working. I knew it wouldn't.

Tuesday

Alison says I'm not trying. That if I don't help myself, there's no point in going on. I don't know where to begin. Boring old Margaret. That's where the problems started. Fancy giving anyone a name like that. Why couldn't I have been Alexandria or Samantha or Georgina . . . something exotic? Maybe my life would have been so much better. I am twenty-four years old and up until two months ago I had a wonderful relationship with Jamie. Bastard! How can I trust another man? Those are tears on the page. I can't go on today . . . just the thought of him.

Wednesday

Couldn't face work today. Rang in and said I had chickenpox, which is going to be hard to explain tomorrow. They know of course. Everyone at school – even the students. Everyone is sick of me. Have to make an effort, have to make an effort. I can't work out what went wrong.

It was a simple error of judgment, nothing more, nothing less. And certainly nothing that cannot be forgiven . . . surely. All I wanted to do was put some excitement back into the situation, throw some chillies in the pot, to speak metaphorically. It's what everyone does. Pick a fight, call off the relationship and then you make up with great passionate sex. Everyone knows that. Only this time I obviously went too far. He didn't want to make it up. He was utterly sick and tired of me, he said. Just wanted some peace.

I'm glad no one can hear these loud racking sobs or see the snot running out of my nose. They would know immediately how completely devastated I am by this whole mess. It serves me right I suppose. It's my fault. I know that. That's why I'm in therapy. Not that I'm crazy, nuts or anything. I'm just totally fucked.

Thursday

Had a bath. Thought about slitting my wrists, but haven't got a really sharp knife. Besides, no one would find me in time, so Jamie wouldn't be able to rush to my bedside and beg to come back. That's more tears on the page. It was just that I went in to work today, said the chickenpox had miraculously cleared up, and Ann the librarian, who had been away for months on study leave, suggested that Jamie and I should come to dinner and meet her new partner. Obviously no one had told her about the split.

'Jamie's dead,' I screamed. 'He was run over by a cement mixer.' There was silence in the staffroom. I don't know what made me say it. It was out of my mouth before I could stop myself. Now everyone thinks I'm totally unhinged.

The principal, Miss McConnichy, took me aside and asked me if there was a problem. Miss White the cookery teacher had informed her of my outburst in the staffroom. I told her I was just expressing myself. Working up some new dialogue for a play I'm hoping to produce with the students. She looked at me rather quizzically. She nodded. I think I got away with it. That's the good thing about being a drama teacher. They sort of expect you to be a little wacky. However, I shall have to watch myself.

I reminded her about my request to use sport time (which I loathe and detest) as a drama club for the junior grades. She said she was still thinking about it.

Friday

Got pissed at the pub after school. Started repeating myself as one does when one is off their face. Jamie stories. I went to the loo and when I came back everyone had gone. I feel suicidal again.

I rang Alison to tell her I felt like killing myself and she suggested that if that's what I really want to do, then maybe I should do it. What am I paying this woman for? Fucking shrinks. They're all loony-tunes. I slammed the phone down – only a slam at my end is still just a click at the other. Anyway, maybe I'll wait till next week to kill myself. Jamie might ring.

Saturday

Watched a romantic movie. Stupid, stupid, stupid. Started thinking about Jamie and how we met. It was at a dinner party thrown by some friends. I had drunk a little too much, which can be a problem. (I mean, I don't mean to, but before you know it, life-of-the-party becomes ugly.) Anyway, I hadn't 'turned' at that stage and was on a roll, making a lot of jokes at other people's expense (which is my forte). But I was sort of showing off in front of Jamie and he thought I was great. Anyway, the subject somehow turned to cancer and I said something really funny. There was dead silence at the table (turned out that one of the guests was in remission – how was I to know?) and I thought it was probably time to leave, as did the hosts, who had already ordered me a cab. But to my surprise this beautiful, beautiful man, Jamie, stepped in and offered to drive me home. I couldn't believe it. And he was straight. I was in seventh heaven. And he thought I was pretty fabulous too. It was like I was in a movie.

We laughed and giggled on the way home in the car, and then he kissed me. Bells rang. And then we made wild passionate love. I know you're not supposed to have sex on the first date but, after all, this wasn't a date. Anyway, in the morning he kissed me again and said, 'You know where this is going, don't you?' And I said yes. I knew. I just knew we were going to be together forever. More tears on the page.

We moved in straightaway and for the next two years it was perfect. We shopped at the markets, went on picnics. We did wild, crazy, romantic things together. We'd make passionate love over a deli lunch (red wine, ham rolls with a couple of olives thrown in). We could have been on a Tuscan hillside. Why am I remembering all this sitting at home alone on Saturday night? It's just making me cry again. I might just sharpen that knife.

Sunday

Went to Mum and Dad's for tea. They are trying to be supportive . . . I think. Bit hard to tell. We don't have that huggy, kissy, let's talk about our problems kind of relationship, which I'm soooo glad about. I'd hate them to tell me all their intimate secrets. Yuk.

Mum cooked her usual grey lamb roast, pressure-cooked cauliflower and bullet-style peas, all piled up on each other like the leaning tower of Pisa. Nothing ever changes. We sat in front of the TV with a tray on our laps. Thank god for television. Some disaster or other on the news. Earthquake followed by jelly and tinned peaches. Out of the blue, Mum suggested that it might be time for me to give up men. She suggested that I should take up a hobby instead. Like gardening. Sometimes I don't know which planet my mother is from. Dad went out to the shed to check on his home brew.

Oh stupid, stupid, stupid . . . how could I be so stupid? Getting ready for bed and looking for a handkerchief in the drawer when I found one of Jamie's old socks. I reached for the phone without hesitation and dialled. Jamie answered. 'I found your sock.' I said. 'You know, the one with the diamond pattern on it that you liked so much. Should I bring it around or do you want to come over and pick it up?'

Even as the worlds tumbled forth, I knew I had gone out on a very dangerous limb. I could hear the sound of sawing. There was silence at the other end of the phone. 'Throw it in the bin, Maggs,' he said, and hung up. Mind you, he didn't have to be that rude. Pathetic end to a pathetic day.

Monday

Had an altercation at school today. I went into the staffroom at morning recess to find a man, who I had never seen before, a man wearing overalls, drinking from my very own personal cup. I could not believe my eyes. 'Excuse me,' I said, 'I believe that is my cup.'

The man looked at me and looked at my cup with, I might add, a certain air of arrogance. 'I'm sorry,' he said, 'but I had no idea.'

I smiled a sort of cold, haughty smile. 'Any fool,' I said, 'with a pair of eyes and the ability to read, would see my name on it.'

He looked at the cup again, he looked under it, around it, all in an extremely showy, pantomimy sort of smart-arsed way. 'Oh,' he said. 'Made in Japan. How do you do.'

I stared at him as he stood there grinning like a monkey. I snatched the cup from him. 'This name,' I said, pointing, 'this name . . .' And then I looked at the cup. But it had vanished. My own personal punchy-machine name which I had carefully stuck on when I bought the cup had disappeared. It must have come unstuck and gone down the plughole at some time or other and I'd never noticed.

I tried desperately to repair the situation to my advantage. 'Well,' I said in a mocking tone, 'everyone knows this is my cup.' I turned to Ann the librarian who had just come in. 'Ann,' I said, 'whose cup is this?'

Ann looked at the cup. 'I've no idea. It's a spare, isn't it?'

The man in the overalls smiled again. 'Well, surely it was an honest mistake then,' he said.

At this point, I detected an Irish accent. 'So you're Irish,' I said.

'That I am,' he said.

'Well in that case,' I said in a suitably demeaning tone,

'I suppose you'll have to be forgiven.'

The man fixed me with the most intense gaze. He had the blackest eyes you could ever imagine. 'I suppose I will,' he said, and went back to reading his paper. I gave my cup a good scrub under the tap, making sure he could see.

'Who is that jerk?' I asked Ann the librarian as we headed out.

'The new janitor,' she said. 'He's filling in for Mr Hedges, who's on long service leave. Quite cute, don't you think?'

'Oh pu-lease,' I said. 'Lift your game, Ann.'

Anyway, I don't know why I've even bothered writing this episode down. Just shows you how tedious my life is.

Tuesday

Alison says that one of my problems is that I take imperfect men and endow them with qualities they never had. Then, when they don't live up to my expectations, I become destructive.

I nodded a lot and pretended to agree, but really, what a load of bat shit. Jamie was already perfect when I met him. I never made up the fact that he was an extremely talented poet and writer. I encouraged him, certainly, and sure, I was disappointed when he took that job with the public service rather than pursue his god-given talent, but it was his choice and I rarely mentioned it. I'm inclined to think Alison has a lot of problems in her own life. She just uses me to try and work through her own angst.

Alison also suggested that I seem to have a very low boredom threshold. She suggested that I should learn to fill my life with activities that don't rely on other people.

That I should learn to enjoy my own company. That there are plenty of things one can enjoy on their own. Like what? Masturbating? I didn't say that of course, Alison would probably have gagged. I'm sure she's the sort of person who does it through her knickers.

She suggested taking up a hobby of some sort – macramé or pottery or sewing, or just pottering around on one's own for the sheer pleasure. I am getting a clearer picture of what Alison's life is like . . . and I notice she's got a moustache. I might just watch and see if it grows any more. Maybe that could be my hobby. She rabbited on and on. God. I am sooo bored. Jamie, pleeeeease come back!

Wednesday

8C are giving me heaps of trouble. Two girls in particular – Sheridan and Amanda. Nouveau riche. Sheridan's father is a wholesale butcher, Amanda's parents own a chain of hairdressing salons. I need say no more. Money, but no class. Their hormones are running wild and all they think about is boys. They have absolutely no interest in doing any sort of work. Their one aim at the moment is to make my life a misery.

Anyway, we were doing a serious job-related drama exercise to give them an idea of what it might be like to work in a bank. It was an experiential situation in which the class divided into customers, bank manager, clerks, the usual sort of situation, filling in forms, asking for loans, etc. Anyway, just as things were working smoothly, Amanda and Sheridan screamed out at the top of their voices, 'This is a stick up,' and ran riot poking their compasses at the other students and stealing all the play money. There was, of course, chaos. I lost my cool. Gave them detention. Riveting day.

Clock ticking on the shelf, gas fire on. I have never been so lonely in my life. I want Jamie to come back to me and stay forever and ever, or I'd like to meet someone else to take the pain away. No. I am not needy. There are just certain things I . . . need . . . (can't find another word, that's all. Will look one up in the Thesaurus later). Am trying to enjoy my own company as Alison suggested but I am just not amusing enough. I'll ring my girlfriend Dana and see if she wants to go out tonight. Somewhere we can meet lots of men.

Thursday

I can hardly bear to write what happened. Oh no. Oh no, oh no, please say it was a dream. Dana and I went to a club. . . All right, I had a few drinks, and maybe that's an excuse for what I did. I went up to this man at the bar, who I can best describe as a poor man's Danny DeVito and begged him to have sex with me. Dare I go on? He said yes, of course, and I took him back to my place.

I turned out the lights when he began to get undressed, but his silhouette screamed *Babe, Pig in the City*. He climbed on top of me like I was an old boot, ejaculated in about four seconds flat, then passed out. I tried with all my might to get him out of my bed, but to no avail. He then proceeded to snore, fart, blow small popping bubbles from his mouth and grind his teeth. I took my pillow and blanket and went to sleep on the couch. But the worst is yet to come.

This morning I staggered into the kitchen to find him still there. Just to be polite I said, 'Thank you for a nice evening, let's do it again some time.'

He said, 'You've got to be joking.' And left.

I rang Alison on her mobile, but she wasn't taking calls.

I left a message to say I needed an urgent session, but she never called back. There's a word hovering on my lips. Desperate. I am becoming a desperate woman. I must fight against it.

Friday

That Odd Job Man is trying to provoke me, I'm sure of it. I had deliberately hidden my cup at the back of the cupboard, but this morning when I swung open the cupboard door there it was sitting up like Jacky, right in the very front. Next to it was another cup that proclaimed in large bold print 'JACK'S CUP – TOUCH THIS AND DIE', etc. With skulls and daggers all over it. Something a two year old would do. I ignored it. I am above such pettiness. He comes into the staffroom like he owns the joint. Mr Hedges the real maintenance man never did that. He knew his place. They're supposed to have little jugs down in their sheds at the bottom of the garden. And he stares at me a lot, as if he knows me, nods to me like we are somehow now good friends. He makes my skin crawl.

Weekend coming up. I think I'll stay in bed till Monday. Or maybe I should clean the house. It's a mess. I have just had a brilliant idea. This is the time. I'll do what Alison says, learn to enjoy my own company. I'll potter around, buy some cocoa, get a video, a good book, cook myself something special, and I'll think positive thoughts. Then I'll do some gardening. The morning glory has all but devoured the back fence. I'll get rid of it. I think I'm actually looking forward to it. A weekend of just me.

Saturday

I have pottered, I have drunk the cocoa, watched the video, cooked my special meal, read the book . . . and now it is pouring with rain. I am totally stuffed. My only other planned activity, the morning glory, has gone up in smoke. And it's only Saturday afternoon.

I rang around to see if anyone wanted to do something. Dana was busy . . . doing what I don't know. I'm sure it was just an excuse. I rang Ann the librarian, but she'd gone out. A girl answered the phone, name of Pauline. Must be her new flatmate. The morning glory stayed put on the fence and grew at least another five feet. It is tenacious. It just won't go away. Too wet to try an eradication attempt.

I wonder what Jamie is doing tonight. How he is managing with only one sock? Is it too early to be best friends with him? I could ring him up and suggest it. Then when we're friends, we could start sleeping together again . . . as best friends do. My finger moving towards the phone. Withdrew just in time.

Sunday

Beautiful autumn day. I leapt out of bed and with great gusto attacked the morning glory. Unfortunately I pulled half the fence down as well. The landlord will be thrilled. Gave up and went to Mum and Dad's for lunch. Dad said he'd help me put up a new fence as soon as possible. 'Don't want to leave yourself open to intruders,' he said. That's the least of my worries, I thought.

Mum has bought herself a new cookbook and decided to experiment. We had some sort of casseroley thing made of fish, white sauce and rice. It was disgusting. I almost craved the lamb roast. Still, at least she's trying.

Monday

Who does this Odd Job Man think he is? This morning when I arrived at school, he had parked his car in my space. I could not believe my eyes. Not that it has my name on it, this space, but everyone knows I have been parking there for the past three years. I am in two minds whether to talk to him about it. I could not handle another challenge in my life.

And later today, I was crossing the quadrangle and I saw him talking and laughing with Amanda and Sheridan. I called them over, chastised them severely and glared at the Odd Job Man, who had the cheek to smile at me. I shivered with revulsion. I can't imagine what they were doing with him. Mind you, rich girls like a bit of rough trade.

Tuesday

Alison says she's concerned that I don't rush the 'healing time'. She is concerned that I might bolt straight into a new relationship for all the wrong reasons. Like, just because I was bored rigid and needed a fuck. She didn't put it like that of course, more that I might have an overwhelming desire for male company and that I shouldn't jump into something I might regret.

It grew, I'm sure it did. Alison's moustache. While I was staring at it, it was actually on the move, millimetre by millimetre. But on a good note, Alison thinks I'm coming along in leaps and bounds. She wants me to continue the diary. Thinks it's working wonders. Perhaps I won't need therapy for too much longer.

I felt quite elated when I left her office. So much so that I drove past Jamie's house. His car wasn't there, so I drove around the block several times . . . well, ten or so times, just in case he turned up. Just so I could wave and say hi, let him see that I am over him. Someone called the police. Thought I was cruising the area. They let me off with a warning.

Wednesday

Went out to dinner for Dana's birthday. There were six of us. We went to an Italian restaurant. God, I hate girls' nights out. No one is really interested in what anyone else has to say. They're too busy checking out the men in the restaurant. As if that's all life is about. Their eyes glaze over when some cute waiter walks past, just as you're making some huge philosophical point about something. Mind you, some of the waiters were very cute and one of them showed a definite interest in me, but I ignored him.

Dana was, as usual, a bundle of misery, because John didn't take her out instead. Some women are pathetic. She has been his lover now for five years and he never turns up on her birthday as he always has some 'family business' to attend to, a fact I pointed out to Dana as she was about to cut the cake. I further added that John was never going to leave his wife and that he was just using her for sex.

Dana, for no apparent reason, burst into tears and, lo and behold, two of her work friends turned on me and said how mean I was, and didn't I ever think about other people's feelings. I was stunned. I tried to point out that all I was saying was the truth. Lucky the karaoke started up or it could have become ugly. I got up and sang 'Raindrops keep falling on my head' and I was the hit of the evening. I think.

Thursday

Sport. Say no more. Only it rained, so we all went into the main hall and watched a movie. Mr Daniels, the vice principal, had his own personal copy of *The Sting*, his favourite movie, on standby. Still, it was better than running around the basketball court. The movie, as always happens, came to a stop halfway through the reel. There were the normal boos and hisses, led by Amanda and Sheridan. General mayhem.

Ann the librarian disappeared and returned with the Odd Job Man, screwdriver and spanner in hand. The girls went berserk as they normally do when any male comes within cooee of the school grounds, but I must admit I was surprised by their enthusiasm. I mean, I suppose if you squint your eyes he is kind of good looking, in a gaunt sort of a way, with those dark eyes and black hair falling over his face. In the half-light, if you had a good imagination, you could almost see shades of Liam Neeson, but he's nothing to write home about. Anyway, just shows you how desperate these girls are.

Will have to make another approach to the principal re the drama club. Cannot bear one more pathetic Thursday of sport.

Had a drink with Ann the librarian after school. She told me that she was gay. I was horrified, but I tried not to show it. Said she'd been attracted to women for as long as she could remember. I think it's just a phase she's going through. I will try and be supportive.

Discovered some small itchy sort of blister things on my vagina. Maybe I should see the quack.

Friday

Oh no. This is too cruel for words. I can hardly bear to put this on paper. Was passing the doctor's this morning on the way to school and thought I'd check out the blistery things. Warts! Vaginal warts! It must have been that man at the club. God is paying me back for being such a slut. The doctor wants me to go to hospital and have them burnt off.

Saturday

Can things get any worse? Decided to stay in all weekend. No point going out with warts. Thought I could try the homey thing again, the weekend of just me, the cocoa, the videos and stuff. Went down to the video store. Lo and behold, I ran into Jamie. He was with Lorelei Jones (who he's known since primary school) and my stomach rolled over in knots. My legs turned to jelly.

Straightaway, I couldn't help myself, I said in a fairly sneering way how pathetic it was to run into the arms of another woman so soon, and Lorelei burst into tears and Jamie said her father had just died and he was trying to be a good friend. 'A likely story,' I retorted.

Jamie looked at me in a severe sort of way. 'Do you ever think of anyone but yourself, Maggs?' And they left together.

As you can imagine, I was stunned. Found out later that it was true about her father dying. Still, I've never trusted Lorelei. With a name like that? I knew about Lorelei, the siren who lured sailors to their deaths on the Rhine. We learned a song about it at school. She's always had the hots for Jamie. Always phoning him up with her little problems. Although, funnily enough, I have never actually met her before today. She always managed to phone when I wasn't there. Went home to bed, warts and all, and stayed there for the rest of the day.

Sunday

Told Mum I had to have some minor surgery. At the hospital. Nothing to worry about. 'It's not warts, is it?' she said. 'Vaginal warts? I've been reading about them in the *Women's Weekly*.'

I lied and said it was an ingrown toenail. Then I had to limp for the rest of the day. Now my leg is sore from limping. Lamb roast was back on the menu. I was grateful.

Got home and wanted to ring Jamie. Boast about the warts. Make out that my sex life is pretty damn exciting. Finger heading towards the phone. Ate a chocolate instead. Not sure this is a good move.

Monday

Detention with Sheridan and Amanda after school over the hold-up business. Caught them passing a note. It read 'WHAT SHE NEEDS IS A GOOD FUCK'. They swore it wasn't about me. I was going to take them to the principal, but I would have had to explain what the note was about.

I began to tell them how disappointed I was in their behaviour, that they were immature and childish. Then the floor polisher started up right outside the door. I couldn't hear myself think, let alone give Amanda and Sheridan a good talking-to. Next came the sound of the Odd Job Man singing at the top of his voice. Some crappy Irish song about Mother McCree.

I called out, 'Excuse me, would you mind turning that thing off.' But he had his back to me and with ear protectors on, couldn't hear a thing.

It was hopeless. By this time Amanda and Sheridan were hooting with laughter. I told them they could go home. They ran out laughing. I walked past the Odd Job Man without so much as a sideways look, as if he didn't exist. I felt him smirking.

Anyway, some light at the end of the tunnel. Miss McConnichy the principal has given the green light for the drama club at sports time. Yippee. I'm quite excited by the prospect. And no more sport to boot. She did suggest that it would be on a trial basis (Sue the phys ed teacher had objected violently), and that to justify the existence of such a club, it might be a good idea to put on some sort of play at the end of the year. Bugger. There go my lunch hours.

Tuesday

Alison thinks I probably overreacted to the situation between Jamie and Lorelei. There are such things as platonic friendships, she said. (I think Alison comes from the same planet as my mother.) She said that it is time to move on. Not to dwell on things. Learn to clear my mind of all those nasty thoughts. She suggested it might be a good idea to sing a little tune each time I think of Jamie, to sort of block him out. 'La la la la la.' I stared at her. 'I know it sounds silly,' she said, 'but it works. Just try it,' she insisted.

Tried it later as I was driving home. I know Jamie is sleeping with la la la la la. He always fancied her la la la la la. He's putting his dick in now as I turn this la la la la – then I hit the gutter and took a great chunk out of my tyre. Think I'll send Alison the bill.

Wednesday

Saw myself in the mirror. I look shocking. Covered in pimples from all those chocolates. The Odd Job Man was banging on some pipe or other with a hammer while I was taking Year 7 for rest and relaxation at the end of class. He is getting right up my nose.

Doctor left a message on the answer-phone. He can fit me in Monday next for the warts. How hideous. There'll be no one to visit me, no flowers, nothing. I can't even tell anyone, it's too despicable.

Thursday

Unbelievable. Talk about scraping the bottom of the barrel. First meeting of the 'Drama Club' today. Every pathetic loser in the school turned up. I am doomed. I am on death row. How am I going to extract any sort of entertainment from this lot? Susan the asthmatic, Brenda the severely weight-challenged, Trudy the moron, Wendy the obviously malnourished from birth . . . need I go on? I tried everything just to get them moving. I'd have had more luck with a cave full of blind wombats.

I started off with a game of 'yes, let's' to get them motivated. 'Let's all hop around on one leg,' I cried. 'Yes, let's', they chorused, but when it was their turn, it was 'Let's lie down on the floor and go to sleep, yes let's.' That was pretty much the end of it. And just when I thought it could not get any worse, Miss McConnichy the principal turned up with Sheridan and Amanda. She had caught them smoking in the toilets and thought as a punishment they could forgo their hockey and be in drama for the rest of the year. Brilliant.

The session was truly agonising. It was painfully obvious that the majority of the group had little if any communication skills, no creativity or even any willingness to do anything at all. They were only there to get out of sport. Except, of course, for Amanda and Sheridan, whose major highlight of the week – bashing other girls' shins with their hockey sticks – had been shafted. And now they were stuck with drama. They hated me more than ever.

Although I cajoled, chided and enthused, it was useless. They were not there to do anything at all. The only successful event of the day was relaxation, but even then Amanda found some excuse to move and in the process deliberately tripped over the weight-challenged Brenda, calling her a 'lard-arse', at which point Brenda burst into tears. By the time the bell went I found myself wishing I was back on the basketball court.

I suggested that the following week they might like to bring in a few ideas for the end of year show. They shuffled off without a word. The only two who were slightly animated were Amanda and Sheridan. They left the hall whispering and sniggering.

Ann the lesbian asked me over for dinner on Saturday night. I couldn't say no. It would look like I was homophobic. So I'm going. Will wear my frilliest frock.

Told Dana, in confidence, about the warts. She laughed herself silly. 'Not that dwarf you took home from the club!' she screamed. 'Serves you right, really.' With friends like her . . . At least she said she'd pick me up from the hospital, which is something, I suppose.

What if I die under the anaesthetic? Jamie would be very sorry then.

Friday

Couldn't help myself. The phone finger went berserk. I tried everything in my power, but to no avail. I rang Jamie and told him I was having major surgery just in case he might be worried where I was. 'Dana told me about the warts,' he said. 'You should be more careful when you have sex with other men.' He said it like it meant nothing. Like he was a friend or a casual acquaintance.

In the background, I heard the clink of glasses. 'Oh, I'm sorry,' I said, 'you've got visitors. I didn't mean to disturb you.'

'It's just Lorelei,' he said. 'She's in a bad way, I'm trying to cheer her up.'

Her in a bad way? What about me? I know he's fucking her. I can feel it in my bones. La la la la la. Why did I ring? Maybe I should cancel the lesbian dinner. Then again, it's something to do and Jamie will see that my car is gone . . . if he decides to drive past.

Saturday

I discovered something amazing under the bed. Doing a bit of vacuuming, trying to fill in time, get in touch with myself, and there it was. A complete microcosm of old memories: an assortment of tissues, old socks, hairclips, a couple of rollers, a tube of lubricant from when Jamie and I were a bit experimental, a condom that was thrown off in gay abandon, *Ulysses* (never could get past the first few pages), earplugs (Jamie used to snore) and fluff, piles and piles of fluff that gave the whole scene a very mystical appearance.

It was like one of those shoe-box worlds I used to make

on a rainy day when I was a kid, with the cotton wool snow, little plastic people and houses, plastic trees, and the coloured cellophane over the top to give it that eerie quality when I looked at it through a hole at one end. I was going to vacuum it, but a feeling of nostalgia welled up in me. I decided to leave it.

Bit nippy today. Think I'll wear jeans tonight instead of frillies. Just hope I don't get molested.

Sunday

Nice dinner with the lesbians last night. I was surprised. Dinner with women has never really been appealing. Spent the whole evening NOT talking about men. It was amazing. We discussed art, politics, theatre, films... It was quite interesting. Ann and Pauline seem to be in love. They were a bit kissy, kissy, which I wasn't mad about. Seemed a bit icky to me. I wonder if I could be a lesbian? Trouble is, I am averse to the female genitalia. That I do blame on Mum – 'don't touch yourself there or a boogieman will eat you' style of thing. Anyway, eating pussy is frankly not my cup of cocoa.

Lunch at Mum's the same, only my brother-in-law (who I don't speak to) was there with my sister and their kids. He is a total plebeian. A plumber. We have nothing in common.

Mum asked if I wanted to hire a TV for the hospital. I said I'd only be in for a day. 'Is that for the *toenail*?' my brother-in-law quipped without looking directly at me. Then he sniggered. I don't know how my sister, who is nice, puts up with him. They've been together for years.

Dad's last batch of home brew has turned out badly and thrown him into a spiral. Something to do with too much yeast. My sister and brother-in-law and kids left straight after lunch and Mum buried herself in her Mills and Boons. She gets a carton of them at a time from a friend. She sits there devouring them one after the other, a cigarette hanging out of her mouth. It is not a pretty sight. Fancy a woman of her age worrying about romance. Surely she knows by now that it's a crock. If we were closer, I'd have a good talk to her, but what the heck. Nearly tempted to borrow one myself.

I watched 'World of Sport' on TV. I quite like looking at those boxer shorts the footballers wear, trying to see which side they 'dress' on. Another riveting day. Still, I've got the hospital to look forward to in the morning.

Monday

Before I went under the anaesthetic, the doctor gave me a lecture about 'safe sex' and sexually transmitted diseases. 'A bit late shutting the gate after the horse has bolted,' I quipped, trying to cheer myself up. He looked at me as if I was a microbe. I don't think doctors have a sense of humour. While I was in recovery, he came to see me. He said that rather than 'spot burn', he'd decided to laser the whole area. Suggested I might feel a little uncomfortable when the anaesthetic wears off. So far so good.

Tuesday

I sometimes wonder if doctors know the meaning of the word 'uncomfortable'. I am in unspeakable pain. I am burning up. My pudendum is hanging down between my knees. Going to the lavatory is like sitting on a pineapple.

I hate doctors. I hate men. Had to cancel my session with Alison. Dana came around with some soup. She had the gall to tell me she'd just had wonderful sex with John all weekend. I pretended to fall asleep. Hope I'm better tomorrow. Have taken too much time off as it is. Alison called to see how I was and said she wouldn't charge me for the missed session.

Wednesday

Shuffled into school, putting on a brave face. I gave everyone the ingrown toenail story, which they seemed to buy. Except, of course, Sheridan and Amanda. Sheridan, who'd apparently had, at one stage of her puny existence, an ingrown toenail, whispered loudly to Amanda, 'She's supposed to be limping, not shuffling around as if she's got something wrong with her twat.' I ignored her. No message from Jamie.

Thursday

Pain settling down a little. Shuffling a little less. That Odd Job Man was raking some leaves in the grounds. He had the nerve to ask me if I was okay. I pretended I didn't hear him. He's still using my car space.

Drama club. Full of dread as the losers lurched in and sat like zombies. I asked them if they had come up with any ideas re the end of year performance. Dead silence. Trying to muster as much enthusiasm in my voice as possible, I then suggested that we could do a tried and true Shakespeare, perhaps *Midsummer Night's Dream,* and began to hand around the books, at which point Sheridan said in a loud voice, 'We don't want to do that shit.'

I controlled myself and said to Sheridan that if this was the case, then perhaps she had another idea. At which point she said, 'Why can't we write something ourselves?' There was a buzz throughout the group, almost akin to a mild form of excitement, and while my instincts said that this was not a good idea – that in fact it usually spells disaster – I thought I'd better go with it. That is, after all, what I'm paid for. To nurture their creativity.

They began to throw around a few ideas. There was the usual serial killer at Summer Bay, teenage witch vampire's revenge, schoolyard massacre and the like (most of these from Sheridan and Amanda), but Susan the asthmatic suggested we could do a Christmas pantomime for the primary school next door. Of course, Amanda and Sheridan bagged the idea, thought it was beneath them, but the other girls outvoted them, so they had to fall in line. I must say I was a little relieved. Not much can go wrong with a panto.

Getting into my car to go home, the Odd Job Man smiled at me with that stupid look he has. Who does he think he is? I ignored him.

Friday

Message on my answer-phone. I cannot believe my ears. It was Jamie. He wants to talk to me. Wants to come over tomorrow. Oh god. He wants me back. He didn't say that exactly, but what else could it be?

I must be cool. He'll have to pursue me with flowers and dinners and champagne. I mean, if he thinks I'm going to fall into his arms just like that, he is mistaken. I'll make a new set of ground rules. Play hard to get. I will not grovel and run around after him. But first I will need to buy a new dress, get some champagne in – French, of course – clean the house, get my hair done, my eyelashes dyed, shave under my arms (haven't done it since he left so it will take a couple of razor loads). I want to look totally amazing when he arrives.

I will need to get up at the crack of dawn.

Saturday

I can hardly begin to write. Oh Jamie, Jamie . . . but start at the beginning. I was exhausted by the time he arrived. Everything was perfect. Just perfect. He never noticed the new dress, the coif, the fingernails, the whipper-snipped underarms, the clean house, the satin sheets. I offered him a champagne and he said no. He was only staying for a minute. He had something to tell me. He wanted me to hear it from his lips rather than from some idle gossip. He was going to marry Lorelei. I could not believe my ears. Daggers fell from the sky like giant shards of glass shredding me to a pulp. He had been counselling Lorelei after the death of her father and, quite by accident, they had fallen in love. They hadn't planned it, it was just one of those 'truly wonderful, amazing, once in a lifetime things'. He never really knew what true love was and now he did. They were getting married in November, and going on their honeymoon to Bali. He hoped that I would wish him all the best. He kissed me on the cheek and left.

I think I am going to vom–

Sunday

Phoned Mum and said I was too ill to come to lunch today. She was disappointed. She'd tried a new recipe, something to do with boiled meat – I dared not ask. Dad wanted to come down and fix the fence, but I put him off. He's worried that an intruder might get in and pillage and plunder. I wish they would!

Called Alison on her mobile. She has agreed to have an emergency session tomorrow night. I have crawled under the bed into my shoe-box world and pulled the fluff in around me and here I will stay for the rest of the day, maybe forever. Thank god I never vacuumed.

This fluff is getting up my nose.

Monday

I can't believe this. Alison was ecstatic. She says this is the best thing that could have happened, Jamie getting married. It means that I can now put him completely out of my mind. I can make a fresh start. It means he is totally out of the equation, so I can get on with my life. I seriously wonder about Alison. She does not seem to have the life experience necessary to deal with this crisis at all. She has obviously not had her heart ripped out of her body and crushed into hot asphalt!

Went around to Dana's after the shrink's. Told her about Jamie. She could not believe her ears. She was in a state of shock. Then she started wondering about the wedding and where the reception might be held and what her chances might be of getting an invite. Lorelei's mother is extremely rich. There would be heaps of free Bolly. It would be the social event of the year.

Dana is so incredibly shallow. I have no idea why we are still friends. Am thinking of moving under the bed full time.

Tuesday

Thought seriously about killing myself today. I figured it might be fitting to jump out of the library window during assembly and go splat on the pavement in front of everyone. But it's only two storeys up and I'm worried I would just paralyse myself and end up having to write with a pen in my mouth and eat through a straw. Not a good look.

I was hovering about the open window when Miss Connichy the principal walked past. Asked after my Aunt Penelope, her old friend from university and my entree into teaching at St Augustine's. Not sure it wasn't a reminder of my somewhat tenuous position at the school. She asked me about the drama group and how it was going. I pretended to be enthusiastic. She then asked me to close the window. I wonder if she guessed.

Worst thing would be, the Odd Job Man would probably be asked to clean up the bits. Need to rethink. Oh, Jamie, it can't be true re the marriage. It must be an icky dream I'm in. Please let me wake up soon. Drove past his house and his car wasn't there. He must be over at la la la la's house, putting his big la la la into her very tight la la la. I am going mental.

Wednesday

Can life get any worse? Took 8C for English today. I was standing in front of the class reading some Blake.

> *I was angry with my friend: I told my wrath, my wrath did end.*
> *I was angry with my foe: I told it not, my wrath did grow.*

I ignored the cry of mock anguish and the muffled 'boring' coming from guess who at the back of the room. This was powerful stuff.

> *And I watered it in fears, Night and morning with my tears:*
> *And I sunned it with smiles, and with soft deceitful wiles.*
> *And it grew both day and night, Till it bore an apple bright:*
> *And my foe beheld it shine, and he knew that it was mine . . .*

I had their total rapt attention. Even Brenda shivered as the pain of the words flowed from every line. I am living it, breathing it.

> *And into my garden stole*
> *When the light had veiled the pole:*
> *In the morning glad I see*
> *My foe outstretched beneath the tree.*

Suddenly there was a crash and a ladder appeared against the classroom window, followed by a head. That dreadful Odd Job Man. He knocked on the window and called out, 'Excuse me, Miss, this will only take a moment. It's the gutter, you see. It's blocked . . . leaves.' With that he climbed further up the ladder, so that only his lower torso was visible, pressed against the glass. Of course the gentle tittering turned into major whooping and screaming. Although he was wearing overalls, he may as well have been standing there naked. The noise was so immense that Miss McConnichy and several staff members rushed in, believing there to be a murder taking place. The room was in an uproar.

'It's that man,' I screamed, 'that Odd Job Man with his genitalia up against the window.' But when I pointed towards the window, there was no sign of him. Even the ladder was gone. And the girls had returned to their books.

The principal called me outside and asked me if I was having problems with class control. I will be seriously watched from now on. I would like to kill that Odd Job Man. He is becoming the bane of my life.

2 am. Something festering in my brain. Some little worm gnawing away. Not sure what it is. Maybe it was reading all that Blake.

Thursday

Drama club got into full swing today. The group began to discuss what they wanted to do in the panto. They didn't want my advice, which was fine by me. I was able to take some time out to think about my own problems. Anyway, they came up with the idea of a princess who is a selfish bitch and doesn't care about anyone in the kingdom but herself, and she gets her comeuppance at the end. I quickly pointed out to them that the protagonist in a story has to be likeable, particularly if she is a female, or the audience will turn off very quickly. A man may be an arsehole and still have everyone love him, but not a woman. (Didn't say arsehole, of course.)

They argued that Joan Collins in *Dynasty* had been very popular on TV. I suggested that if that was the way they wanted to go, they would have to make the princess amusing or the audience would just be bored. 'And how, may I ask, does she get her comeuppance?'

'Well, we don't know yet,' said Amanda. 'This is a work in progress.'

At least it's keeping them quiet. Gave me time to think.

2 am. Jamie, Jamie, Jamie. I am sooo horny I would almost welcome being spirited away by a spaceship and given an anal probe.

Friday

Another weekend looming in front of me. Got out all the poems Jamie wrote for me. Read them again . . . How is it possible for someone to write all that stuff and then fall out of love so quickly? I don't understand.

> *Your lips are like the sunlight falling on sheaves of wheat,*
> *The warmth of you calls me, caresses my very soul*
> *You are my light, my love, my heat.*

I mean, you can't just say those sorts of things and then dump someone. Surely. Maybe I should go around to Jamie's and point that out. Or better still – should have thought of this before – I could go over to Jamie's parents place. Pay a visit. We always got on well. Haven't talked to them since the split. Say I'm just passing and drop in for a coffee, see what they think about the whole situation. I'm sure they'll be on my side.

Saturday

Jamie's mum seemed quite pleased to see me, although she did have to go out pretty much straightaway. Jamie's father was also late for a game of golf and was dropping the younger kids off to friends. They all left, so I drove home.

Rang Jamie when I got back to tell him his family seemed to be in good spirits, all healthy and well, just in case he wanted to know. He said he did know as he had seen them only last night, when they met Lorelei's mother to discuss the wedding. Oh god. Did I need to know that? My heart is breaking in two.

Sunday

Mum and Dad came over. Dad wanted to measure up for the fence. He is still worried about intruders. I am more worried what the landlord might say about destroying his property. 'You can't be too careful,' Dad said. 'There are some very nasty people around these days.' He suggested I buy a dog. That's actually not a bad idea. I could lavish all my wasted love on him . . . but then you have to feed them, wash them, pet them. Maybe it's not such a good idea after all.

I thought that I'd cook Mum and Dad a special lunch, perhaps give Mum an idea of what food should (a) look like and (b) taste like. Cooked a very nice curry and fluffy rice. Dad complained that it was too spicy and Mum wondered why I hadn't put any pineapple in it. Still, Mum got stuck into the ironing and Dad mowed the lawn for me. At times like this, it's great to have parents.

School tomorrow. I can hardly wait – ha ha. It just goes on in an endless cycle of torture.

Monday

Something is going on with that Odd Job Man. Last period of the day I went to the library to see Ann the lesbian, only she had gone home sick. Anyway, I thought I'd stay there out of the way, in case there were any extra classes to be taken. Looking out the library window, I could see the Odd Job Man raking leaves near the main gate. All of a sudden, a large black car with tinted windows pulls up and the driver's window slides down. The Odd Job Man goes over to the car and has a conversation with the driver, who I couldn't see from that distance. Then the car drove off.

What is he up to? There is something not quite right about him. I feel it in my bones. He is up to no good.

Tuesday

Alison says that sometimes when adults are having difficulties in their lives, particularly when they repeat patterns in their relationships, they need to find the root cause. What I need to find is a root, forget about the cause . . . cheap joke. Anyway, she suggested that a lot of problems come from childhood experiences. I knew this was coming. 'Well,' I said in a sort of gloating way, 'that doesn't apply to me. In fact I had a very good childhood, excellent in fact. I was spoiled rotten, got everything I wanted.' She began jotting down notes at a rate of knots.

I started thinking about Alison at that point. Tried to imagine her having sex. Would her moustache get in the way? Did she cry out in passion or lie there like a mute? Had she ever *had* sex? I suppose she must have as there is a photo on the desk of a couple of kids. And her husband doesn't look too bad, which is surprising as Alison is fairly plain, a bit like a chubby Camilla Parker Bowles, but the mad prince can't get enough of her. I wonder if she gives good head? I wonder if she swallows? Not that I'm big on that myself. Find myself gagging on the odd occasion.

Alison was still rabbiting on. 'Are you taking this in, Margaret? It's very important you do.' Alison clucked and nodded and kept writing. I leaned sideways, trying to read her notes: 'obsessive . . . destructive . . . attention-seeking'. I wondered who she was writing about and how dare she spend time on another case, when I'm footing the bill!

I was so glad when the session finished. It was the most tedious one of all. Alison then asked me a strange question. 'Who is the Odd Job Man?' I must admit I was very surprised. When I asked why, she said I had mentioned him a few times.

'That's because he's driving me crazy,' I said.

'You're not attracted to him, are you?' she asked.

I laughed like a drain. 'Oh pu-lease. He's a janitor.'

'Well,' she said, 'a lot of nice people are janitors. In fact my father was one.'

Now I see where Alison's problems are coming from.

Wednesday

Keeping my eye on the Odd Job Man. Still suspicious about him. It's a certain look he has. And I wonder why he always takes his shirt off when he digs the garden? I mean, this is a girls' school after all. All that sweat running down his body, making his singlet stick to his six-pack. It is so obvious he is just trying to get attention. I watched him for fully half an hour, just to see what it is he's up to.

Thursday

The drama club's progressing nicely. I advised them to look for a strong premise in the story. They came up with 'pride goes before a fall'; I suggested that they map out the personality of the princess, give her a history. If she's going to be a selfish bitch, what made her that way? Was there some tragedy in her life? Was she bitter about something? Did she have an awful childhood?

Amanda asked if she might have just been born that way — maybe she had inherited a 'bitch' gene. They all thought that was hilarious, of course. I intimated that it might make her a very shallow character, but it was up to them. In any case they would need to take the character on a journey of growth and change. I said 'sea change' but that went over their heads like the Concorde. 'The princess would have to see the error of her ways,' I explained. That set them off into a frenzy of chatter and exchange of ideas. They are very excited.

The best thing about it all is that they don't seem to want my help. Means I can slack off a little. They are working well, I have to say, although there is a lot of whispering and sniggering between Amanda and Sheridan, but I ignore it. I feel myself freeing up in a lot of ways. I think the diary is helping. Maybe I'm ready for another relationship.

Driving home in my car I caught a glimpse of Amanda and Sheridan outside the local milk bar talking to guess who? He is such a sleazebag. Probably a paedophile.

Friday

Ann the lesbian has asked me to a party on the 15th. Don't know whether I could hack it. All those dykes. But it's her birthday so I couldn't refuse. I wonder if I should ring Jamie and ask him. Say it was an old invitation and that both of us were asked because Ann didn't know about the break-up and it would be quite rude of him to refuse. He had met Ann several times so it seems only natural I should ask him, now that I think about it. And he liked her a lot, as I recall, so he might be really upset if he found out she was having a party and I hadn't invited him. Only he wouldn't be able to bring Lorelei, because it's a special occasion, and if he wanted to get a lift with me that would be okay, or pick me up, or I could even pick him up if he couldn't remember where Ann lived, which is possible because he's never been to her house.

It's times like this you can see as plain as the nose on your face that THIS DIARY CRAP ISN'T WORKING. I wrote it down like Alison told me. It was all there in front of me in black and white. And the logic of the argument seemed to be quite sound. It seemed on paper to be the only thing to do. But if I'd taken more time perhaps I would have seen there were certain flaws in the scheme. I wouldn't have rung and therefore would have been spared the humiliation of him reminding me that he was busy with wedding plans and wouldn't be able to go and certainly not without his fiancée, Lorelei. Oh shit.

Maybe I should ring him back now to explain that I wasn't ringing to try to get him back, because I am completely over him as it turns out. I don't want him to get the wrong impression. It was just a genuine concern that he might be upset that I hadn't mentioned Ann's party, and I didn't want to spoil our special friendship.

OH GOD, I DID IT AGAIN! I made that second call. I couldn't help myself. Why, why, why? Maybe I should ring him back just one more time to tell him that I have my period and I'm a little unhinged because . . . someone died, someone I was really close to – no, that sounds like Lorelei . . . say I was in fact seriously ill, they had found a worm in my brain, and the doctors told me I only had a day or so to live and I needed him to come straight over. No . . . that's not going to work. I'll think of something.

Thank god the phone was engaged. Been engaged now for an hour. Two hours later, still engaged. Maybe he hasn't put the receiver back on the hook properly. I wonder if I should go over there, let him know the phone is off the hook, just in case there's an important call waiting or an emergency of some sort?

Saturday

Couldn't write any more out of pain and anguish.

Turned out Jamie had taken the phone off the hook to save me the humiliation of calling again because he was trying to be kind and Lorelei was there when I arrived. She'd just been looking at wedding dress books and her mother was there and said how sad it was that my house had burned down and what was I going to do. Lorelei intimated to her mother that I had a screw loose and I mentioned something about her being a used car salesman's daughter and she called me a loser and I called her a grasping superficial slut who had wrecked my life . . . And the whole thing got completely out of hand and Jamie had to step in between us.

'It must have been totally amazing,' screeched Dana. 'I wish I'd been there. I wonder if they'll postpone the wedding. Is she going to press charges?'

'She hit me first,' I insisted. But I can't really remember. Another bad day at Black Rock.

Sunday

Roast pork for lunch. I think. There was some crackling, which was the only clue. I wasn't hungry anyway. I had flashes of Jamie and Lorelei fucking . . . the la la fucking la la is not fucking working. I could see them groaning and writhing on the bed. Naked, sweaty, hot. Mum interrupted.

'Come on, cheer up, love, can't have you sitting around with that morbid look on your face,' she said. 'Oh,' she added, 'I ran into Jamie down the street. What a nice boy he is. Pity you couldn't have kept him. Mind you,' she said, 'I knew it wouldn't last. And his new girlfriend is so nice, and so pretty – except for that black eye.' La la la la. I cannot stand it. I am going mental. I need to see Alison urgently.

Monday

'What am I paying you for?' I screamed at her. 'This is just money down the fucking tuberonies. I've done the diary, I've tried the la la la, it's all a load of crap. My love for Jamie is growing. I cannot live without him.'

Alison did her best to calm me down. 'You've had a minor setback,' she said. 'That's to be expected, but you're doing very, very well.'

'What a load of cods,' I sobbed. 'I have never been so unhappy in my life.'

'Look at all the positives,' she said. 'You've got your health, you have your job . . . what you need to do is concentrate on other things, take an interest in other people. There is too much concentrating on self,' she said. 'You have to work harder. Find a project that you can throw yourself into.'

I wanted to scream out, why don't you either wax your upper lip or grow a handlebar moustache, but I didn't get a chance because Alison was on a roll then. She gave me the impression she had pretty much had it up to pussy's bow with me. And I'm not a cruel person, deep down, so I bit my tongue.

'You are your own worst enemy,' she went on. I mean, what a thing to say to a distraught patient. All this blame willy-nilly on my head. What about everyone else? Is it my fault that Lorelei took Jamie away from me? Is it my fault that Jamie is treating me like shit? Is it my fault that my life is in such a mess?

'Pretty much,' said Alison. I was totally wrung out after our session. Maybe this is what I need. A good yelling-at. Maybe I should ring Jamie and tell him I am well on the road to recovery . . .

Tuesday

Now that Sheridan and Amanda are in the drama club, I thought there might be an attitude change in class. I was sorely mistaken. I had decided on another experiential type of situation. A simple shopping trip to the market – not that either of them have to do their own shopping, but just in case they fall upon hard times and the servants can't go, I thought it would be fun.

The students adopted the roles of stallholders who'd come down from the country with produce, and city folk who wanted to be supportive because of the drought etc. Conversations arose about the weather, what it was like to live in the country versus the city, and some interesting arguments got under way. That is, of course, until Amanda and Sheridan ran in with padding tied around their waists under old raincoats they'd found in the costume box, and screamed out that they were suicide bombers and would blow the market and everyone in it to bits. The room descended yet again into its customary chaos and Miss McConnichy the principal and Miss White the cookery teacher rushed in to calm the situation down as some of the girls had run out of the room and were hysterical.

Miss McConnichy took me aside and once more challenged me on class control. I suggested that Amanda and Sheridan were the ones out of control and that I was going to send a note home to their parents letting them know that the two of them needed reining in. She agreed that both girls could be a trial at times, but reminded me that their fathers were building the new school library, so perhaps we should treat them a little more gently.

What a joke. Who is the victim here? I thought about sending the letters anyway. As luck would have it, though, who should I run into at the bottle shop after school but the butcher's wife and the hairdressing magnate – Sheridan and Amanda's mothers, respectively, both obviously straight from the gym in their Armani tracksuits and joggers. The butcher's wife sported a fake leopard skin coat, false eyelashes and red fingernails. The hairdresser, still with the blue rinse under her fingernails, wore a fur coat that could have been a hairy nosed wombat for all she would have cared. The butcher's wife, Rachel, had a trolley full of gin and the hairdresser, Skye, was pushing a load of bourbon.

I introduced myself and they remembered me from the one parent/teacher night they'd ever been to. I eyed their trolleys as they tried to explain they were stocking up for a party they were throwing. I believe I hid my disdain as well as possible. When the butcher's wife asked me how the girls were going at school, I had my opportunity at last.

I suggested that Amanda and Sheridan were making a mockery of their education, that maybe they'd be better off not bothering. And I got them where it hurts: the money they were spending on the girls' education could be better spent elsewhere. Not only were they poor achievers, but they were disrupting the other students to boot. Maybe I went too far, but I was in the mood. Both women nodded. I'm sure it went over their heads, the idea of an education of any sort being a foreign concept to them. I'm sure they were lucky to reach Year 8 themselves. Both, however, said they would take the matter in hand.

Wednesday

Late for school. Turned into the driveway to find a huge truck blocking the entrance. Waste paper. I tooted the horn and, lo and behold, that fucking Odd Job Man with his grinning dial popped his head around the corner of the truck. 'Be with you in a minute,' he said.

'I don't have a fucking minute,' I screamed. 'I am late for class, get out of my way now.'

He came right up to the car, leaned in the window and said. 'If you ask me nicely, I'll see what I can do,' and then he walked away.

I stared at him. How dare he speak to me like that! 'You fucking moron,' I screamed, and with that he disappeared behind the truck. I was out of the car. 'You,' I screamed, 'the truck – move it.'

He smiled at me. 'Nicely,' he said. And turned his back on me.

I have never been so insulted, but time was of the essence.

I gritted my teeth. 'Excuse me,' I said, biting my tongue, 'would you mind moving the truck? I am late for class.'

He turned around and smiled again. 'Of course, Made in Japan. I'll move it for you right away.' He signalled to the driver of the truck to move and then obsequiously ushered me through. I am going to kill that man.

Called into the office. Miss McConnichy not happy that I had gone against her wishes and spoken to Amanda and Sheridan's parents. Both had apparently rung the school for more information re their daughters' lack of performance based on what I had told them at the supermarket.

'It's all true', I said to Miss McConnichy. 'They are a menace to the other girls.'

Miss McConnichy argued that they were just imbued with youthful folly and enthusiasm, and to have spoken to the parents without permission was against school policy.

I am stunned. I am the victim here and once again I have been targeted. What is going on in my life? Anyhow, the upshot is that Amanda and Sheridan have both been grounded by their parents till the end of the year. No parties, no boys, no frivolous sexual encounters, no nothing. Perhaps that will make them come to their senses.

Thursday

Disastrous day at drama club. I was greeted by total silence. It seems that Amanda and Sheridan have got the nerds onside re them being grounded. I tried to explain that I was doing it for their own good, that in fact they would thank me later in life for nipping their uncontrollable behaviour in the bud. No response. Couldn't even get them to warm up.

I tried pleading, cajoling, even humiliating contempt, but to no avail. Then I suggested that they all might like to go back to their various sports. Amanda and Sheridan ran straight through the door, but the others looked at the wintry conditions outside and decided to cooperate. We managed to get some ideas flowing.

Near the end of the session, Miss McConnichy brought Amanda and Sheridan back in. She had found them in the toilets, fagging on again. Amanda and Sheridan stood at the back of the hall, sullen and resentful. They'll get over it, I'm sure.

Friday

I am shaking so much I can hardly write. Oh my god. Oh my god. Am trying to pull myself together. I'll just get a drink. Back now. Start from the beginning. Set the scene. A huge storm, lightning flashing, thunder rumbling, rain bucketing down. Stayed back after school to catch up on my assessments – and I thought I could suck up to Miss McConnichy, show her that I am a diligent teacher . . . Anyway, it was a dark and stormy night. Well, afternoon. And it appeared that everyone else had left for the day, so it was pointless me staying. I decided to go home.

Not having taken heed of the storm warnings on the morning news, I was without an umbrella or suitable coat, but it was only a short distance to my car and I ran through the mud. When I got there I found my car listing in a pool of water. One tyre was as flat as a pancake. I went back into the office to call a taxi, but I couldn't even get through. I called road service, but the wait was over two hours. I decided to try and hail a cab outside the school or, if worse came to worse, catch a bus.

With a piece of plastic over my head, I ran down the gravel drive, which was full of puddles. I saw a bus at the bus stop. I ran, but before I got there, it took off. A taxi passed by driving through a huge lake caused by a blocked gutter, sending a tidal wave over me. I was in total despair. Why has my life turned so sour? Behind me came a car with its headlights on. The car horn tooted. Assuming it was one of the staff, I ran over, opened the car door and got in. It was not until I was inside the car that I realised who the driver was. It was the Odd Job Man – grinning at me, like a spider sitting in his web, and I, the poor butterfly with sodden wings and shaggy hair, caught.

I tried to get out of the car, but it was already moving. I was suffocating, I wanted to throw up, but I didn't want him to see that I was affected in any way by his presence. 'Lovely weather for ducks,' he said. How pathetic. How banal. I didn't even bother to answer.

'Where to?' he said.

'A taxi rank will be fine,' I replied.

'Oh no,' he said, 'I wouldn't dream of doing that. I wouldn't send a dog out on a day like this. I'll take you home. Where do you live?'

'It's out of your way,' I replied.

'How do you know that?' he said. 'You have no idea where I'm going.' He smirked at me. Not that I was looking, but you can feel when there is a smirk in someone's voice. 'So,' he said, 'what suburb is it?'

'Hawthorn,' I muttered.

'Hawthorn, eh?' he said. 'This is your lucky day. I just happen to be going that way.' And with that he put the blinker on and we turned left.

'So,' he said, 'do you have a name? Can't keep calling you Made in Japan, can I?'

I was trapped, cornered. 'Margaret,' I squeezed through my pursed lips. 'Margaret Anderson.'

'Jack,' he said. 'My name's Jack, in case you wondered.' I didn't bother to reply. 'So, Maggie,' he went on, 'what is it you teach?'

'I'm a drama teacher,' I announced rather grandly.

'A drama teacher?' he replied. 'Ah yes. Of course. I've seen you running around in the hall playing games, pretending to be this or that. What the fuck does it teach you about real life? It's a complete load of shite!'

I was struck dumb. This . . . Odd Job Man – Irish to boot – daring to suggest that my chosen profession was a waste of time. I turned to him in a slightly patronising, sneering way and said, 'And that is the astute, educated observation of a janitor, is it?'

He looked back at me, catching me in his hard, almost cruel gaze. 'Ah,' he said, 'only a complete fool would judge a book by its cover, wouldn't you agree?' At that point I turned away, shaking my head in a haughty, 'I will not deign to continue this conversation' sort of way.

We had just pulled up at a set of traffic lights when, without warning, he yelled at me to 'get down and stay down'. Then he grabbed my shoulder and pushed me forward as far as the seatbelt would allow. He put his foot on the accelerator and, wheels spinning on the wet road, screeched over the median strip, through the oncoming traffic, and started speeding in the opposite direction.

Of course I started screaming for him to 'stop the car, stop the car at once', but to no avail. He just kept speeding on, over gutters, around corners, up laneways, sideswiping rubbish bins . . . It was just like in the movies, only this wasn't a stunt, this was really happening. One hundred k's, two hundred k's, unbelievable. At one stage the car left the road and became airborne. We were flying! I was terrified. My mouth was wide open, but there was no sound coming out.

The car finally screamed around a corner on two wheels and into a laneway. It screeched to a halt. He undid my seatbelt and pulled me over to the driver's side. 'Don't make a sound,' he whispered. His grip on my body tightened. I could feel my heart pumping. I could smell the sweat on his body. I was totally captive in his arms. He listened, he watched . . . the minutes ticked by. Suddenly he let me go. Then he started to laugh.

I stared at him. 'Who was chasing us? Where did they go?' I blurted out.

'Who was what?' he laughed.

'Chasing us?' I screamed. He looked at me as if I was crazy.

'There was no one chasing us,' he said. 'I was play-acting. Workshopping an idea.' He looked at me with that stupid grin on his face. 'Had you going there for a minute. Look at you with your bright eyes and rosy cheeks. Livened you up a bit, eh? More fun than you've had in a while.' With that he started up the car and took off.

I was in such a state of shock, I could not speak. When he eventually pulled up outside my house, I ran in without looking back. Inside I leaned against the doorway. I caught sight of myself in the mirror – the flushed cheeks, the bright eyes, the wild hair.

Funny. I can only mention this to you, dear diary, but I feel a tad excited. My flesh is tingling and – dare I say it? – I am strangely turned on in an odd sort of a highly sexual way. No no. This is sick. I will not succumb to something so ridiculous. Mind you, I may have to masturbate just to go to sleep.

Midnight. Drugs! I should have thought of it earlier. This was no joke. This was no workshopping. That chase was for real. There was someone after us. We were in danger. It all adds up now. Oh yes. That would explain everything – the black car at the gate, the chase . . . The Odd Job Man is a drug dealer. Of course. It's a perfect situation (now that I come to think of it). Exclusive girls' school, young indolent girls with plenty of money to throw around. Yes, yes. But what to do? Should I call the police? Go straight to the principal? I am at a loss.

2 am. Still awake. Can't get the Odd Job Man off my mind. Trying to remember all those movies I have seen where people are in this situation. Most of them get blown away. I will have to be very, very careful with the way I handle it. But I know this much, he's not going to get away with it. I will sleep on it. Maybe the answer will come tomorrow.

Saturday

Morning. Hardly slept a wink. Knocked myself off several times to try and tire myself out, but to no avail. Dad came over and changed the tyre on my car. Thought I looked particularly perky for a Saturday morning. Asked if I did something special last night. Didn't say anything. Had to tell someone, though, so I went over to Dana's. She sat there with her mouth open as I told her the story. 'So, did you fuck him?' she said.

I stared at her incredulously. 'What?' I said. 'How could you say such a thing?'

'Well it's obvious he was trying to get into your pants,' she said.

I could not believe my ears. 'He's the school janitor!' I exclaimed.

'So?' she said. 'You weren't too fussed when you shagged that dwarf from the club.'

'No, no,' I said. 'This is something bigger, this is something big-time. This man is evil incarnate. I believe he is . . .' I paused long enough to suggest that I could hardly bear to part with the rest of the information, which caught her attention as I knew it would. Then I lowered my voice dramatically: 'I believe he is a drug dealer.'

'Oh,' she said, 'if that's the case, maybe you could get me a few tabs of ecstasy at a good price.'

I could see there was no real point in continuing the conversation. This was going to have to be my own private fight.

Dana could not see the considerable dangers. 'So what are you going to do?' she said.

I sighed. 'No idea. But I will not let him get away with it.'

We opened a bottle of wine.

'At least it's keeping your mind off Jamie,' she said.

I laughed lightly and long. 'I am so over Jamie it's not funny,' I said. 'In fact I can't think what it was I saw in him. I just realised how much time I had wasted. I should have seen it from the beginning . . . in fact, now that I think about it, he is quite repulsive.'

'Which reminds me,' she said. And then she hit me with the sock full of sand: 'I was at the mall the other day and guess who was there? Jamie and Lorelei. And you know what? She's really nice. Such a gorgeous face, and what a body. No wonder Jamie is hooked,' she said. 'Her skin is like silk and those eyes . . . and so intelligent too.'

'Intelligent?' I said. 'What are you talking about? She works in a perfumery.'

'She's assistant manager,' said Dana defensively.

'She's a shop girl, for fuck's sake,' I said. 'She serves behind a counter. Any dumb-arse can do that.'

'I don't think that's fair', said Dana, who works in retail herself. 'She has other qualities.'

Stupidly, I said, 'Like what?' Then she went on and on about Lorelei's immaculate hair, her manicured nails and her superb taste in clothes. The pain began in my toes and started rising until I screamed out, 'Why don't you fuck her yourself?'

'I thought you were over Jamie,' she quipped. 'Sounds to me like you're still in love with him.'

I denied it vehemently, but deep down I know she is right. What a fucking disaster. Everyone knows that you marry someone who is on an equal footing. That's the way matches have been made since the beginning of time. Kings didn't marry peasant girls. Sure, they shagged them, but they always married within their rank. It has to be a meeting of minds in every possible way. Jamie – cultured, intelligent, writer and poet – with a girl who serves in a perfume shop? I don't think so. I know her family is rich, but how did they make their money? Selling used cars. I mean, what is going on here? Where is the meeting of minds in a social context, like Jamie and I had? We could have the most amazing sex, then discuss politics, art, literature, a whole variety of subjects. What's he going to talk about with Lorelei? Floral bouquets versus the musks, or perhaps an in-depth discussion re whales' vomit?

Went around to Jamie's. Felt the need to enlighten him about the error of his ways. No one home. He's probably over at the Rhine slut's place and they're probably going at it hammer and – la la la . . .

Sunday

Went to Mum and Dad's. Curried sausages. With pineapple, of course. I think Mum was trying to show me, in a kindly way, that her version of curry was much more acceptable to the palate than mine. I was tempted to point out that the curry should be fried in with the onions, not added from the packet just before serving, but I was too depressed. Dad thought it was delicious and suggested I get the recipe from Mum in case I was having a dinner party. I said nothing.

Tried to keep my mind off Jamie. Engaged Mum in a conversation re the political situation in El Salvador. She nodded a lot and then picked up one of her romance novels and began to read.

Harder. Have to work harder. Nothing is working. My love for Jamie is growing. I cannot live without him. Maybe I should neck myself. Hang myself from the light. Problem is, all the lights in the house are those old pull-down ones. My feet would be on the ground before I turned blue. No, I will not be defeated.

'What you need to do is concentrate on other things,' Alison had said. 'Take an interest in other people. There is too much concentrating on self. You have to work harder. Find a project that you can throw yourself into.' Maybe a quest of some sort. Something to take my mind off the whole situation. There's the panto of course, but that's hardly stimulating. There's Alison's moustache, but that's hardly riveting either, and I only get to see it once a week.

Now, the Odd Job Man . . . all that business with the car, the man at the gate? He'll take my mind off Jamie. I'll expose him to the world for what he is – a paedophile drug dealer. I'll be a hero and exalted by all for saving the girls at St Augustine's. Their innocence will be intact. I'll have my name in the paper. Lots of people, including Jamie, will see it and I'll be adored and worshipped by all and sundry. So how to go about it? Need to concentrate and think of a plan. Have to use diplomacy, tact and, above all, take the upper hand in the matter of exposing him. I am almost looking forward to it.

Monday

In retrospect, maybe I handled the situation badly. My plan of action was to engage the Odd Job Man in a conversation about nothing in particular and then, with my superior intellect, trick him into making a confession. I have no idea why I thought it would work. Shit.

It was like he had vanished into thin air. There was no sign of him. He wasn't in the staffroom at morning recess, or lunchtime. I knew he was at school because his car was once again parked in my spot and I heard the sound of the ride-on mower somewhere out on the grounds. I was beside myself with anxiety. I had to put an end to this once and for all. I was duty bound.

In my spare period after lunch, I decided to go looking for him. I set out across the oval to the other side of the school where the gardening sheds were situated. I had forgotten how huge the school grounds are as I crunched through the fallen leaves, through the dense undergrowth. I suddenly became aware of how very alone I was. If I screamed, no one would hear me. Fear crept into my heart. I decided to turn back.

As I turned around, my foot got caught in the undergrowth and I stumbled into a gully that was full of water. I fell forward into the bog, my hands sinking to my elbows in the mud, while one of my shoes disappeared into a black hole in the ground. I bent down and reached into its murky depths, feeling for my shoe, when I heard a sound behind me. Before I could turn around (I was on all fours at this stage), I felt a pair of strong hands gripping me around the waist and lifting me up out of the boghole. I turned and stared in horror. It was the Odd Job Man.

He placed me gently down on the ground. He stared at me, his black, black eyes piercing my soul. There was a strange smile on his face. 'You better get that off.' His hand reached towards me as if to feel my breasts.

'Don't you touch me,' I screamed and pushed his hand away.

'Leech,' he said. I looked down and there was this big black slug thing crawling up my blouse. I screamed again, and clawed at my blouse like a madwoman. By now I was a little unhinged. All my cool had gone out the window as I flicked the leech off.

'Are you okay?' said the Odd Job Man.

'I'm fine,' I hissed. 'Just fine. And guess what?' I added triumphantly. 'I know what you're up to. You're a drug dealer, aren't you?' I blurted.

'What?' he said, staring at me in a bemused sort of way.

I went on: 'It all adds up. That business in the car on Friday. You were trying to get away from someone.'

'It was a joke, I told you,' he retorted.

'Ah,' I said, playing my trump card, 'then how do you explain the man at the gate? The man in the black car. I saw you.'

He stared at me for a moment or two. Then he began to laugh. He could hardly speak from laughing. 'The man in the car? The black car at the gate? He was asking directions.'

'What?' I said.

'He wanted to know where the supermarket was.'

'You expect me to believe that?' I screamed.

He pinned me with a cold hard stare. What happened

next I can hardly put into words. In fact I need a drink right now.

Hate having to squeeze the bladder from the cask. Must remember to get some proper wine tomorrow. Just another sip. Right. Set it down on paper, as Alison says, then you can work it out . . .

Without any warning, he grabbed me by the shoulders, drew me towards him and kissed me hard on the lips. The urgency of the kiss bruised my mouth and yet there was a softness, a gentleness I can't explain. For the briefest moment his tongue pressed between my lips into my slightly open mouth. And then he let go.

I was, needless to say, totally stunned. I reeled back, gasping for breath, and then I hit him across the face with all the energy I could muster. The blow bounced off his gaunt face without him even flinching.

'I deserved that, Maggie. I'm sorry.' He was as cool as ice. 'Now,' he said, 'about the drug dealing, let's sort this out right away. I assume you have proof, so let's go and call the police, shall we?'

With that he started heading towards the school. Bluffing. I knew he was bluffing. But what if he called the police? I couldn't prove anything. I could be charged with being a nuisance or something. I rushed after him and grabbed him by the shirtsleeve. 'There's no need to call the police,' I said. 'I just wanted to let you know . . . that I know.' And with a pathetic 'This is just a warning, that's all,' I turned and left him with my head held high, carrying my left shoe in my hand. I could feel his black eyes boring into my back. I was shaking from head to foot. My legs were like jelly. I could hardly walk.

But worse than that . . . I can hardly bear to think about

it, let alone write it down . . . my twat was wet. Sexually aroused. I could hardly believe it. Had to go to the loo and use some tissues.

Tuesday

Told Alison what happened. She began blowing her nose a lot. Tears were rolling down her cheeks. She must have been strangely moved by the story. At length, she suggested that maybe I had overdramatised the situation and that I should try and look for the best in people, not the worst. She believed I had allowed my rather fertile imagination get the better of me.

Didn't tell her about the kiss or the wet bizzo. Didn't want her to get the wrong idea. At the end of the session she pointed out that I had not mentioned Jamie once, which was a major leap forward she felt. So I drove by Jamie's house afterwards just in case he was out the front. I wanted to tell him about my success in getting over him, but the lights were out.

Wednesday

The Odd Job Man bounced into the staffroom for morning tea, cup in hand. I turned my back and ignored him. The next minute he was leaning down, whispering in my ear, asking me how the investigation was proceeding. He smirked, then sat down with Pamela Goodwin the art teacher and they chatted and laughed until the bell went. How she can lower herself like that I don't know.

Anyway, I can now put this whole ghastly mess out of my mind. I never have to speak to that turkey again and it is absolutely certain that I will never, ever accept another lift in his car. Even if there was a pack of wild dogs snapping at my heels. Thank god for that.

Thursday

Drama club going AMAZINGLY well and the most enthusiastic of all are Amanda and Sheridan. Surprise, surprise. They have, it seems, accepted the error of their ways, accepted that their grounding was not my fault but a result of their own misdemeanours. They have turned a corner. I am off the hook.

Group decided to call the panto *The Foolish Princess*. We began to improvise the story, sort out the characters. And most of the ideas came from them. So far we have a kingdom where everyone is unhappy because the princess is a bitch.

'Why is she a bitch?' I asked them. They decided that it was because she couldn't find a husband.

'Why can't she find a husband?'

'Because she's a total cunt,' Amanda piped up.

I sent her out for ten minutes.

Sheridan continued with the tale. The princess thinks she's better than everyone else and doesn't accept she has faults. She will get her comeuppance in the end. That's as far as we got. Not a bad start . . . a moral tale.

Miss McConnichy thinks the panto is an excellent idea and has already informed the primary school next door about the end-of-year show. I am in the good books.

Friday

There is something wrong with this picture. There is something so totally fucking wrong with this scenario. I am rigid with rage. I can hardly bear to put pen to paper. I was supposed to have dinner with Dana, but she cancelled because John had a weekend pass from his wife, so I got dumped as per usual. Decided to go over and give her a piece of my mind, tell her she should be supporting her friends in their hour of need.

When I pulled up in the car, I was surprised to see Jamie's car out the front. I nearly vomited there and then. I could think of absolutely no reason why he would be at Dana's except to ask her advice re his coming back to me. My legs turned to jelly. Oh joy, oh every prayer answered.

I started hyperventilating as one does when one is overwhelmed by the anticipation of an overwhelming event. Luckily I had a bag on the back seat to breathe into. I've seen lots of medical shows on TV. Although maybe it's meant to be a paper bag, now I think about it, not plastic. Sucked it in so hard I nearly suffocated on the spot. But it did the trick, because I got such a fright when I had to fight for breath, when I couldn't get the plastic out my mouth, that it sort of calmed me down. Just the thought of dying like that brought me to my senses.

I was not sure how to approach the situation. I crept around the side of the house. I heard voices and I peeked around the corner. There, to my horror, was Dana and John with Lorelei and Jamie, playing happy couples, laughing and drinking, sausages sizzling on the barbie, all having a good time as if there was nothing wrong. My best girlfriend entertaining my ex with his new girlfriend when there had hardly been any period of mourning.

I turned and began to run back to the car, but

unfortunately Dana's dog Rover saw me and bounded after me, humping my leg as he usually does, slowing my progress and causing me to trip and fall into the rose bushes. Then he began humping my head. Think he may have come a bit in my hair. Oh, humiliation mounting on humiliation.

3 am. The worm is coming, it's eating its way to the surface of my brain. I am not going to take this lying down. I have let them all pour shit on me and haven't said a word. Enough is enough. I am not going to be cuckolded by that slut from the Rhine. There's no fury like a woman who has been fucked over by her lover and her best friend. Rage is filling my heart. The wedding is not going to take place by hook or by crook.

Saturday

Still in my dressing gown. Just stopping to have a drink. Am reading all the literature I can on REVENGE. Fascinating. Acts of homicide, of cruelty, of public humiliation, torture, depravity, madness . . . so many choices. Laying out your victim on an ant hill or tying them to a post in shallow water and letting the tide come in so the giant crabs can nibble on them, or sending wilted roses, dead fish, casting spells. Oh yes. The worm has definitely turned.

Decided to play it cool. Went over to Dana's and pretended nothing had happened re her total betrayal of our friendship.

'Is this yours?' She waved a scarf in my face. 'You must have dropped it when you peeked around the corner last night. Everyone knew it was you,' she said. 'And you should stop encouraging the dog. He was so excited that he barked for the rest of the evening and kept pushing his lipstick out.'

I challenged her about her deceit.

'Why should I stop seeing Jamie just because you broke up? We always got along well, and Lorelei is very rich – nice,' she corrected herself. 'So very nice, and her mother has just given her a pale blue Audi sports car. It's amazing. We all went for a drive.'

I was nearly gagging by this point, but I controlled myself. 'Perhaps I should get to know her better,' I lied. 'I could do with a new friend. Where does she live and what's her phone number?'

Dana looked at me with suspicion. 'You're not going to turn into a bunny-boiler?' she asked.

'Furthest thing from my mind,' I declared. 'No, I just want to understand her better. It will help me get over Jamie if I know he's going to a nicer person.' Luckily the dog ran in just then and started humping my leg. Dana, distracted, wrote down Lorelei's address and phone number. Eureka.

2 am. Watching that old movie *Gaslight*. A diabolical plan is forming. I will drive her mad, although it will be difficult to turn her gas up and down, but maybe the electricity? I could cut a wire and black out her house . . . then again, I'd probably end up electrocuting myself. Not a good move. Needs more thought.

Sunday

Went to Mum and Dad's for lunch. Baked mincemeat in a loaf. Why would you bother?

Went out to Dad's shed while he was on the loo after lunch and checked out all his tools in case I was hit by a brainwave re murder and mayhem, only I ended up jamming my finger in the vice and didn't know which way to turn it to get free. Dad, as usual, came to my rescue. Think I will lose my fingernail.

Monday

Another run-in with the Odd Job Man. After class Amanda and Sheridan asked me who was going to help us with the lighting and sound, build the sets etc, for the panto. 'We're only girls, after all,' she said. Admitted that I hadn't really thought about it.

Amanda ran for the door. 'I'll ask Jack. He'll help us.' And she disappeared. 'Go after her, Sheridan, bring her back. I do not want any help from that awful man,' I screamed. 'He is an imbecile!'

Only he must have been passing at the time because suddenly there he was, with that ridiculous grin on his face, standing in the doorway. 'Oh well,' he said, 'in that case, do it yourself,' and he left.

'Now what are we going to do, Miss?' yelled Sheridan. 'He was our only chance. There's no one else in the school that can do the job.'

'Don't worry,' I said. 'I can do it.' I don't know why I said it. I barely know how to put a plug in a socket. Shit.

Thank god, Ann the lesbian said she would help with the show. Do the music. Unfortunately she wasn't any help re the sound/lighting/building problem. 'Ask Jack,' she said, 'I'm sure he'd be happy to help.' I said nothing. Ann reminded me about the party next Saturday. Asked me if I was bringing anyone. Forgot all about it. And worse still, no one to ask. If I could just find a plan, get rid of Lorelei, I could take Jamie to the party.

Watching old movies again. *Dial M for Murder*. Of course . . . The phone . . . I shall make a phone call. Or several in fact. I will ring Lorelei at home every ten minutes. I will not let her get a wink of sleep. She will be tormented and demented, but more than that she will look like a total dog. Bags under the eyes, she will be cranky and snappy. Jamie will freak when he sees her. This is a truly cool plan. I will keep her awake all night. Finger heading to the phone now.

Not sure how it's going. First couple of times Lorelei answered it. I did the breathing bit and some screaming, a few obscenities – normal stuff. Well, I think so, seeing I've never done it before. After a while she didn't answer the phone at all, but that has not deterred me.

3.30 am. I have been ringing every ten minutes since ten o'clock. She will be distraught, she will be off her head. Mind you, I'm nodding off myself.

Tuesday

Late for school. Felt like shit.

Alison asked me about the bags under my eyes. Wondered if I might not be sleeping well. 'You're not staying up all night making lewd phone calls, are you?' she joked. Alison is right onto me. It's uncanny. 'Revenge is such a shallow thing,' she rabbited on, 'it's something that only weak people indulge in, because it gets you nowhere in the long run. Once someone's feelings have changed, there is no amount of cajoling that will bring them back. You can send letters, yell, scream, threaten, but it won't change anything. It's too late. You are just hurting yourself. That's why you need to move on. Celebrate your own life. This is what I've been trying to say to you.'

I must have started snoring because the next thing I knew, Alison was shaking me. She sent me home to get some shut-eye. Hope she isn't going to charge me for the session. Hope she didn't say anything important while I was nodding off.

Eureka. There's a phone message from Jamie. He wants me to ring. Oh my god, it has worked. I will just have a glass of wine first. I want to savour the moment. Lorelei has obviously had a bad night, looks like shit and he has discovered how awful she is.

I'll ring now.

Jamie says if I don't stop making nuisance calls the police will be notified. Apparently Lorelei went over to Jamie's after the first couple anyway. Jamie suggested I might need some help. Have I thought about seeing a shrink?

This is Alison's fault, I can see it as clear as day. If the therapy was working, I wouldn't have to be humiliated like this. Maybe I should get a new shrink, or at least ask for my money back. But I can't waste all this energy on negative thoughts. I just have to think of something else to tear them apart.

Wednesday

I know he's up to something. There is something so incredibly evil about the Odd Job Man, something Machiavellian, something rotten. There was a car at the gate again. I'm sure it was the same car. Well, it was a dark colour anyway. I should have got a registration number but unfortunately I was taking an English class with 8C. I watched him chat to the driver for some time. He looked up at the window and waved. Must have guessed I was watching.

I didn't hear Sheridan sneak up on me. 'I bet he's got a big one, Miss,' she said. I looked at her in horror. She's fourteen years old. I told her off. She feigned shock, said she was referring to his 'spade'. When I gave her detention, she said she'd love to stay but her father was having dinner with the principal re the new library and she had to help her mother.

What a load of crap. They have servants. If Sheridan has ever lifted a finger to help anyone, I'd be very surprised.

Thursday

The panto plot so far: the selfish princess, who we are calling Patsy, is making life miserable for all the people in the kingdom because she is so mean. The king and queen believe that if she met someone and fell in love it might change her ways and she would become a nicer person. They bring princes from all over the world, but the princess always finds fault with them and has them thrown into the dungeon or whatever, and as a result is twice as mean to her subjects. Her subjects get together and decide it's payback time.

There were several ideas about what should happen

next, but nothing suitable. Amanda, as predicted, suggested that we just throw the princess off the castle wall into the moat, where the crocodiles could maul her to death. I suggested that perhaps the princess should learn some sort of lesson, see the error of her ways. I told them that all fairytales have morals. Amanda queried that by screaming out, 'What about Goldilocks? She stole all the bears' food and got away with it.' Then of course she started doing bear things — ravaging the others, biting a few legs. I had to physically restrain her. Maybe she has lesbotic tendencies.

No one had a clue as to how we could punish the princess. I told them to write some opening scenes. I suggested that out of this effort maybe the inspiration would come.

I also informed them that Shakespeare often opened with the premise of the play in his first speech. Which of course led to Amanda suggesting the opening line should consist of a villager screaming 'Let's get the bitch.' I pointed out that the children we would be performing to were only five and their parents might not appreciate that sort of language. By the end of drama club, the first scene had fallen into place.

PRINCESS: I'm so booooored. I need someone to entertain me. Where is the court jester?

(*Court jester appears.*)

PRINCESS: Tell me a riddle. Something really funny so I can laugh till I puke all over the floor and someone slips in it and falls flat on their face.

Guess who wrote that line?

COURT JESTER: What's the best thing to put into a Christmas pudding?

PRINCESS: Your teeth. I know that one, you stupid moron. Off with his head.

(*Courtiers grab the jester.*)

KING: But, sweetheart, that's the fourth jester this week. There aren't too many comics left in the kingdom.

QUEEN: Yes, darling, be fair. We need all the laughs we can get.

PRINCESS: Oh all right. Just a damn good flogging then.

COURT JESTER: You're so very kind, your Princessness.

(*They drag him out.*)

QUEEN: Now, we have four very nice princes who have arrived from countries near and far. Perhaps you might like to marry one and be very happy.

PRINCESS: Pigs might fly.

(*Sound of Ann playing a trumpet fanfare.*)

KING: Here they are now…

(*Enter four princes.*)

KING: The young Prince of Farthingland.

PRINCESS: (*screams*) Too fat. Have an elephant sit on his head.

KING: Prince Edward from Nanoland.

PRINCESS: (*screams*) Too thin. Throw him into the alligator pond.

QUEEN: But darling –

PRINCESS: Are you questioning me? Take Mother to the gallows, have her drawn and quartered, then her guts spilt out and burned.

I suggested that might be too much for the littlies.

PRINCESS: Next?

KING: Prince Albert from the mountains.

PRINCESS: Too tall – let the wolves chew on his leg . . .

KING: Prince Brendan from Iceland.

PRINCESS: Too short – stretch him on the rack.

(*She laughs and rolls around on the ground.*)

KING: This can't go on. She's making everyone's life a misery.

QUEEN: We have to do something. We need to teach her a lesson. But how?

Good start but, as I said to them, where is the plot going? We need to put something into place before the end of term. Amanda asked me again about the sound/lighting. Am going to have to suck up to the Odd Job Man at some stage. My skin crawls thinking about it.

10.30 pm. Just about to go to bed when it suddenly hit me. The way to win Jamie back is to make him jealous. Find a new man and flaunt myself in front of him. Oh yes. Perfect, perfect . . . Jamie will go berserk. He will be unable to contain himself. He will drop the Rhine slut and come running back to me. But who will I use? Who is tall, dark, handsome and really likes me?

Oh yes – Larry. Jamie's best friend from school. He's been living in San Francisco. Just arrived home a couple of weeks ago. He is gorgeous, and he adores me – he rang after the split and commiserated with me. And now I come to think about it, he is bound to be Jamie's best man. I'll be able to pump him for info re the wedding. Perfect. I will call him in the morning, ask him to the lesbian's party. Yippee. Kill several birds with the one stone. Hope he doesn't fall in love with me.

Friday

Re approaching the Odd Job Man about sets etc. Think I might have blown it. I was alone in the staffroom, washing my cup, when I heard the door swing open. I turned around to see who it was and suddenly I was face to face with him. He moved to the sink and was standing so incredibly close, I could feel the heat from his body. It was deliberate, of course. He was trying to make me succumb to his manliness. I nearly gagged, but stood my ground. If only Dad had taught me more about carpentry I wouldn't have been in this situation.

Anyway, he moved in, reaching for a cup, a hair's-breadth away. I could feel him breathing. I could almost feel the blood surging and pulsing through his body. But I remained completely cool, although for a brief second I did start thinking about, of all things, what his penis might be like, how big it might be, was it circumcised or not and whether or not it would fit in my mouth, but I'm sure that was just a reaction to Jamie . . . in some way . . . a subconscious jealousy thing which I can't at this point explain. Might leave that now.

He broke the silence. 'Tea?' he said.

'Thank you, no,' I said, coolly. 'It seems,' I then said carefully, 'that it may be a good idea if we try to work out our differences.'

'Is that because you have a production and you're going to need help with the sets, lighting and the sound?' he said.

I forced a smile. 'Of course not,' I said, 'the thought hadn't even crossed my mind.'

He moved in a little closer. 'Really?' he smirked. 'So what did you have in mind?'

There was an unfortunate throbbing in my twat. So loud you could almost hear it.

'Perhaps we could . . . meet one night. After school.' I was really floundering now, mainly because the blood had drained from my brain. 'For a drink, to see if we can't resolve the situation.'

'Is there a situation?'

'I just don't want there to be any . . . unpleasantness,' I said. I know it sounded pathetic . . . and it was.

'Fine by me,' he said. 'Tell me where and when.'

At that moment Pamela Goodwin the art department tart, came in. Because the Odd Job Man was standing so close to me, the stupid look on my dial could easily have been misconstrued as hot-twat face, the kind you get when you have totally succumbed to your passions and there is no turning back, you are pathetic and your legs are about to give way. Not that it was happening of course, I was concerned Pamela might have thought there was something untoward afoot, so I pushed the Odd Job Man away, calling out loudly, 'If you come near me again, I'll have you up for sexual harassment,' and stormed out of the room.

Shit. Bad move on my part. Doesn't really solve the lighting/sets problem.

After school he was emptying the bins as I came around the corner. There was no escape. He laughed out loud as I went past. 'When I sexually harass you, Maggs, you'll really know about it.' What was that supposed to mean? There goes the twat again. I think I might have to go to the doctor's. There's something wrong with me. Maybe I'm incontinent. And why is he calling me Maggs? That's what Jamie used to call me. Is he being deliberately cruel?

Rang Larry. He is coming to the party with me. Oh joy, oh wonder . . . oh happy day. He was a little reticent at first, maybe because he owed some loyalty to Jamie or something, so I assured him that it wasn't a date as such, I just really wanted to see him again and also I was sure that he would enjoy the company of the people attending the party . . . I laid it on pretty thick as one does when one is really on the make but wants to assure the other person they are not.

Anyhow, he seemed pleased. He said he was sad to learn that Jamie and I had broken up. 'C'est la vie,' I said. Think he believed me. But the best bit of news is he's having lunch with Jamie on Sunday. This could not be better. We will have a fab time Saturday night – who knows, we may make mad passionate love – then he will be smitten, unable to control himself. He will tell Jamie that I am the most wondrous girl in the world. This is the happiest day of my life. By Sunday night Jamie will be mine.

Saturday

Didn't tell Dana who my date was, but I gushed and swooned. She was extremely curious. Turns out she's going to be at the lunch with Jamie tomorrow. Not sure how she managed an invitation, but I didn't ask. I will be able to pump her about what happens. What his immediate reaction was, and how emotion overcame him. I said that I was over the moon about my date. He could be the one. I must admit I laid it on pretty thick, but these are desperate times.

Bought a new dress, which is so hot, new haircut, new follow-me-home-and-fuck-me shoes. Larry is picking me up at eight.

Sunday

I am never, ever getting out from under this bed. I plan to stay here for the rest of my life, nestled into the fluff with this cask of red. When my body dies and my soul has gone to heaven (if one believes in that shit), I will become part of that fluff, a part of the dust of life. It will be as if I never existed . . . all my thoughts will have disappeared into the ether. I will have become one with the universe . . .

I had gone to so much trouble. The new haircut looked great, the dress was to die for (skin-hugging black strapless) and the shoes (which, I must admit, I was tottering in) showed off my legs to advantage. I noticed that with the stress of the Jamie break-up, I had lost a little weight and in fact my previously ordinary body had acquired a few curves.

I was a tad nervous before Larry arrived. It had been a year and a half since I'd last seen him, and I remember him being extremely handsome but, now, who knows? Someone could have thrown acid in his face since then. I'm not sure I could cope with scars . . . I had a couple of drinks and the doorbell rang.

Larry looked amazing. More gorgeous than I remembered. And he'd obviously been working out. His body was spectacular. He had on a pair of tight leather pants, tee shirt, designer jacket. Perfect. This was going to be an evening to remember. As he followed me down the hallway to the living room, an idea formed in my head about how the evening would go. We would stay at the party for a couple of hours, be pleasantly pissed, then come back to my place and fall into bed with wild abandoned passion. He would leave sated in the morning and head to Jamie's for lunch, where he would have that wonderful after-glow of sex written all over his face... and everyone would ask what he'd been up to last night. Jamie would be on the phone by four o'clock in the afternoon, begging to see me. By four thirty he would be mine. It was a perfect plan.

But something was wrong. I couldn't put my finger on it until Larry, having gushed for fully ten minutes about my dress, insisted on rearranging my hairstyle. It was pretty much set in stone when he started screeching about my shoes, asking would I mind if he tried them on, his boyfriend would just adore them.

I stared at him. My mouth opened like the entrance to Luna Park.

'I thought you knew,' he said. Apparently he'd come out of the closet when he was in San Francisco. He'd met this guy called Freddie and fallen head over heels in love.

I almost gagged. 'I had no idea you were a huge screamer,' I blurted out.

'It doesn't change anything, does it?' he asked. 'I still wanted to see you, to tell you about my new life, and catch up. You did say it wasn't a date.'

What could I do? I wanted to scream out, what are you talking about, you big poofter? I wanted you to shag me so Jamie would come back. But how could I say that? It would have seemed like I was using him.

Obviously he could see the disappointment – nay, devastation – written all over my face. He apologised and said he would understand if I didn't want to take him to the party.

'Don't be silly,' I lied. 'In any case it's a lesbian party. It should make you feel at home. You'll be amongst your own people.' But I asked him, just for the sake of the evening, to please try and pretend he was straight and that he was my boyfriend. He thought that would be an absolute hoot. Being a big butch boy again. He would be delighted. No one would ever know, he promised.

I should have said no, there and then. But how was I to know how things would turn out?

(There is someone knocking at the door. I peeked through the window. Mum and Dad, Mum with a casserole. I pretended I wasn't home. After a while they went away.)

At the party Ann greeted us at the door. I introduced her to Larry, my new boyfriend. She was very pleased. Glad to see that I was moving on in my life. He tried – he really did try – but it started to go pear-shaped when we went into the bedroom to deposit our coats. The bedroom was decorated in purple and pinks and Larry started gushing over the decor and the fluffy cushions, and the screeching and handwaving started. He sighed over the crystal punchbowl, swooned over the wallpaper in the hallway, and felt faint at the marble in the kitchen.

'I just luuuuve your taste, girlfriend. It is sooooo me!'

Ann looked at me a little surprised. I kicked Larry in the shins and he managed a 'g'day, mate' and a 'how's it going then, buddy?' in a very deep voice, but it was clear that it was going to be a big ask.

As luck would have it no one else had arrived yet. I jostled him into a corner and ordered him to stop being such a huge wus. We had an agreement, he had promised me – on his word of honour. Of course, he was devastated. He hadn't meant to go over the top. He would try really, really hard. I felt a little mean, but it passed very quickly.

Guests started to arrive. Lots of dykes, and then teachers from school. I introduced Larry to all of them as my new boyfriend, and he was doing well. He put his arm around me, was laughing with a deep voice, slapping me on the bum like we might have an intimacy of some sort. He had come into his own. I had won. He talked about cricket and football and car racing.

And then – horror of horrors – who should arrive but the Odd Job Man. I could not believe my eyes. He was with the slag from the art department. She was all over him like a rash. He was wearing a tee shirt and tight jeans with a huge bulge at the crotch. I nearly gagged. How obvious I thought. Larry, who had seen him, whispered, 'Oh my god, look at the size of that lunch.'

'It's socks,' I said, 'a pair of socks. Now for fuck's sake, get a grip on yourself. You're butch, remember.' He apologised profusely. 'Stay here,' I ordered him. Then I dragged Ann into the kitchen. 'What is he doing here?' I hissed.

'Who, Jack?' she said. 'I asked him.'

It was out of my mouth before I could stop myself: 'But he's the janitor.'

Ann, who is very politically correct, looked at me with a degree of disdain. 'So what?' she said. 'He's a nice guy. You should get to know him.' As if . . .

I hurried back into the other room to find Larry chatting to – or should I say, up? – Barry Day, the science teacher. I hurried him away. He apologised profusely again. He said this wasn't working out. Maybe he should leave. 'Just try a bit harder,' I said. 'It's really important.'

I could see the Odd Job Man looking my way, so I hissed at Larry to kiss me. Larry closed his eyes, took a deep breath and kissed me.

Jack came over. 'Well,' he said, 'didn't know you were coming. Like your hair.' Larry had stopped in his tracks. He was staring at Jack, starting at his crotch then moving his eyes slowly up every inch of his body towards his face.

'This is Larry, Larry, this is . . .' I swear I couldn't say his name without gagging.

Jack butted in: 'Jack,' he said. 'How do you do, Larry. I'm the janitor at the school.'

At this, for some god only knows reason, Larry started to drool. Drip, drip, drip onto the polished boards . . . 'That must be nice,' he said. 'I suppose you wear overalls all day?'

Jack moved in close to Larry. 'Oh yes, I do. With a tee shirt. It gives me room to move when I do all that physical work.'

'What about when it rains?' said Larry, his chin now wet. 'I suppose the tee shirt sticks a bit.'

'Oh yes,' Jack said, 'sticks to my shoulders, to my back –'

I interrupted in a loud voice: 'Darling, could you get me some punch, please?'

'What?' said Larry, who was almost in a trance.

'Some punch, my love,' I said, my smile hiding clenched teeth.

'What punch is that?' said Larry.

'The punch in the punchbowl in the kitchen.' I kicked him hard in the shins. He came to and wandered off, his head still in the clouds.

'We're so much in love,' I sighed at Jack. 'Larry and I.'

Jack grinned. 'Really?' he said. He moved in close. 'Does he give good head? And who's on top? That's what I want to know.'

I stared at him with the sort of stare that says, you are so gross and pathetic, I won't even deign to answer.

'Because I'm thinking,' said the Odd Job Man, moving in closer still, 'that Larry might be batting for the other team.'

I stared at him with contempt. 'At least he doesn't have to put a pair of socks down his trousers,' and with that I swept off. I had won. I had got the last laugh, so to speak.

I met Larry coming back with the punch. I downed it in one gulp. It was pretty strong. Larry was swooning. 'Oh my god, that man is beautiful,' he said.

'Your taste must be up your arse,' I snapped.

'Oh yes, absolutely,' he said, 'as far up as possible,' at which point I nearly gagged. I was totally grossed out, so I reached for another punch, and then another.

Mr Garbageman had headed back to that slag from the art department and the two of them were laughing, probably at my expense. The evening was heading downhill at a rate of knots, but I was determined to have a good time. More punch was the answer.

Ann came up to me, I think, and suggested I slow down on the punch. Something about there being a lot of vodka in it. 'I'll be fine,' I said, and headed back to the lounge room, just in time to see Larry trying on the curtains. That was the last straw.

I turned the music up and started dancing. Larry began leaping around the room like a young faun from *Giselle*, so any attempt at heterosexual pretence was now down the gurgler. My head was spinning by then, so I don't remember too much after that, though I do recall dancing on the table top . . . showing my tits, I think . . . yes. But nothing else too horrible. Except . . . my arse . . . the map? Did I show the map of Tasmania? Not sure, but there's something stirring in the recesses of my brain . . .

Oh no, please don't let it be true, please say it's a dream . . . Oh no. The memory is flooding back as I write. For some reason I was heading out the door – Ann must have called a cab – and then . . . oh god . . . I ran back into the lounge room, put my hand down the Odd Job Man's trousers and screamed out, 'See – it's a pair of socks!'

Only it wasn't. *Ahhhhhhhh* . . .

Rock bottom. I am at total rock bottom. I have no recollection of what happened after that. I hope nobody tells me.

There's nowhere I can go from here. I will call an emergency session with Alison tomorrow. She has got to help me. This is all her fault. If the therapy was working, it wouldn't have got to this.

I can hear someone knocking at the door. I'll just pull the fluff in. I may never leave this dark space again.

There is something else tormenting me. A huge question mark hovering over me. I don't have a clue what happened after a certain point. What did I do? How did I get home? I woke up naked in bed, with my clothes neatly folded on a chair. It must have been Larry.

Phone ringing. Let the answer machine pick up. It is Dana. She is laughing so much she can hardly speak. I am glad I am amusing somebody. Larry obviously told some story at the lunch. Once again everyone amused at my expense.

Monday

Monday bloody Monday. Knew that if I didn't go to school today, I would never go back. Dragged myself out of bed (alcohol pimples all over my face) and headed for school.

Suddenly I remembered that Ann had hired two of the senior girls to be waitresses on Saturday. Those little trollops had probably been hot on their mobiles all day yesterday. But as I entered the schoolgrounds, nothing untoward was happening. The two girls in question, Isabel and Natalie, passed by with their usual 'good morning'. Maybe they had left before I disintegrated.

In the staffroom I did notice a slight halt in the conversation as I entered, but nothing was said. I did not detect sniggering of any sort. Pamela the art slut kind of smirked when she asked me how I was feeling, but that was it. I had gotten away with it. Maybe everyone had been as drunk as me and my behaviour went unnoticed.

But it was not to be. On entering my 8C English class I found Amanda on top of the desk, dancing in a lewd manner, lifting her school jumper up and screaming out, 'Sock it to me, sock it to me.' At this point Sheridan was poised to plunge her hand into god knows where and pull out god knows what. They froze. 'Just practising for the play, Miss.' This, no doubt, will be their excuse for anything from now on.

Worse was to come. I was called into the principal's office. Word had apparently reached the ear of Miss McConnichy. She expressed concern about my behaviour out of school hours, which I suggested was really none of her business. A parent of one of the girls who was at the party had rung and questioned my suitability as a staff member of this very exclusive girls' school. My protests that I was writing a book about a seriously tormented soul – a sort of Dante's inferno-based project – and I was just living through the character, fell on deaf ears.

Regardless of her affection for my dear aunt, she indicated that my position at the school might need to be reviewed. I needed to set an example when there were students present. She could not afford the slightest hint of scandal amongst her staff. However, she agreed to let me off with a warning to 'lift my game'. Our meeting was interrupted by Miss White the cookery teacher, arriving with the morning tea. Scones and jam and cream. Miss McConnichy, who is bordering on the corpulent, began slavering at the tray and I was summarily dismissed. For some unknown reason I started thinking about Miss McConnichy's sex life – ew.

On the way to class, I saw the OJM pushing a wheelie bin towards me. I darted into the girls' toilets. Not sure if he saw me or not. I have to work out a way to never ever have to see him again, which is going to be pretty hard to do if I'm going to have to ask him to help with the panto.

In my first spare period, I rushed to the library. I apologised to Ann. Asked her if I broke anything. She thought it was all pretty funny. She hadn't had such a good laugh in years. Thought I was the life and soul of the party. Thank god for people like Ann. Nonjudgmental. Only a week to go till end of term. Will I make it?

Dana called in after work on the pretence that she was concerned about me. She wished she'd been there, as a friend of course, to help me. She went on and on about the fabulous lunch with Jamie and Lorelei and how Jamie had been appalled at the story. Then she mentioned that Larry had arrived late at the lunch. Apparently he'd gone off with one of Ann's male friends and shagged all night. So much for true love, I thought.

'But that's okay,' I said. 'It's all right for a bloke to be outrageous, but not a woman. Guys can do anything they like and screech and laugh about it the next day. What happened to equality of the sexes?' I concluded.

'So the pants incident is true,' she said. 'It wasn't a sock after all. Larry said his dick must have been huge!'

Trust Dana to care not about my humiliation, nor my angst and torment, but about the size of the Odd Job Man's member.

A final blow for the day – a call from Jamie. He had, of course, heard about the party. He was calling to suggest I seek urgent psychiatric help. He was concerned that I had totally lost the plot with my life. He was sorry for whatever part he might have played, but he couldn't help me anymore. Larry had obviously regaled everyone with a detailed account of the evening.

'Did he mention trying on the curtains?' I asked. 'Slavering all over the school janitor?'

Jamie suggested I try not to point the finger at others for everything that goes wrong in my life.

Just after he hung up, I started thinking very seriously about everything. Why is my life such a shit heap? Why is everyone out to get me? Alison. This is the problem. Alison. I have now spent hundreds of dollars on therapy and has it worked? No. It is time to put the blame in the right place.

Tuesday

I'm not sure exactly when Alison's seizure began. Maybe I did come on a bit strong, telling her she had totally stuffed up my life, that the diary was a stupid idea, and finally suggesting some depilatory wax for her upper lip if she couldn't hack electrolysis and for fuck's sake do something with her hair.

She went rigid in her chair and gave me a really weird look.

'I need some answers here!' I yelled. 'That's what I'm paying you for, aren't I?'

Slowly she got to her feet and pointed a finger at me. 'You want some answers?' she said. 'All right. You are the most . . . you are the most . . .' Her voice started to quaver at this point.

'The most what?' I shouted.

And then it happened. At first I thought she was waving her arms in celebration, the truth of the moment exciting her. But when she reeled backwards over the chair, I guessed this was more than just paroxysms of joy. She hit the carpet, I screamed, and the building's security guard rushed in.

He turned Alison on her side, made sure she wasn't biting her tongue, and called an ambulance. He asked me if I could stay for a few minutes while he fetched a blanket.

I sat staring at Alison, all quivery on the floor, and experienced an odd sensation. Not in a lesbotic sort of a way, but I felt . . . I don't know, something . . . compassion is too strong a word. It'll come to me. I stared at that plain little face. It suddenly occurred to me I knew absolutely nothing about this woman who had been guiding my life for the past few months.

Then again, I'm the one forking out the money, and shrinks aren't supposed to tell you about themselves. The security man returned. He said Alison's husband was coming and I could go. He would wait with Alison. So I left.

Outside in the cool air, I headed for the car. A thought suddenly occurred to me. I had been cast adrift. I was like a cork bobbing on the sea of life. I was totally . . . on my own. What the fuck was I going to do? I needed Alison to help me. And more importantly, what was it she was going to say? You are the most . . . what? Amazing? Beautiful? What was it that threw her into that fit? I just hope she will be back on deck next week.

I drove my car around to Dana's place. I needed to talk to someone. I could see the yawning chasm of my life opening up in front of me. I knocked on the door and called out that I was desperate, that I needed refuge from the storm. She yelled, 'I'm in the middle of a shag. Go away.'

Drove past Jamie's house and saw him pull up in the car with Lorelei. Suddenly couldn't face him. Then I drove to Mum and Dad's. Maybe I could share my problems with them. Decided against it. Mum would only tell me to take up gardening again.

The dreadful thought suddenly hit me. In the whole universe, there was no one who wanted me, who loved me . . . except Mum and Dad, I suppose, in a parental sort of way, but the bottom line is, I had no one. How could I manage alone? And what was it Alison was trying to tell me?

Wednesday

Message from Alison's husband saying that Alison was taking leave for a couple of weeks. I could not believe my ears. What am I supposed to do in the meantime?

There was an emergency number which I rang. I could hear Alison in the background. Not sure why she didn't want to take the call. I told her husband, who sounded very nice, that Alison had been trying to tell me something when she had her seizure, had been trying to give me some sort of message. I was the most something – could he ask Alison? He told me to hold on for a minute, and then came back. 'Alison says to go back over the diary,' he said. 'Read it all. There will be a clue in there. You must find it yourself as this is a journey of self-discovery.' Then he hung up.

Well, I have read and reread it, but I can't find anything in there pointing the way to any epiphany. I am the most . . . What? Extraordinary? Intelligent?

One comment in the diary suddenly struck me: 'Larry arrived late to the lunch.' He had been shagging that friend of Ann's. Maybe I'm being paranoid but, if that's the case, if Larry was with someone else after the party, who drove me home? Who undressed me and put me to bed? Must have been Ann.

Thursday

Dilemma. Huge. In drama club this afternoon I thanked Ann for taking me home, sort of joshed that I hope she didn't finger me or anything . . . Ann laughed, thinks I'm funny. Then she hit me with the awful truth. 'I didn't take you home,' she said, 'it was Jack.'

Oh fuuuuuuck. He had apparently found me on the

floor in the bathroom with my cheek on the tiles, had lifted me up and carried me to the car. So who undressed me? Ann shrugged. 'You'll have to ask him,' she said. 'Anyway,' she continued, 'I'm glad to see you two are friends, we're going to need Jack.'

I went into a total state of shock. Could not think of anything more revolting – nay, repulsive – than the garbage-man taking my clothes off. I might have been sick there and then but my thoughts were interrupted by Sheridan, who was leading a drama warm-up that consisted of dancing around drunk, falling down with your cheek on the floor and passing out. She said it was a new form of Tai Chi. Tried not to think about it for the rest of drama club.

Amanda and Sheridan wanted to do a punk rap number as the opening song.

> *Mean as cat shit, mean as puke,*
> *The selfish Princess would kill you for a look.*
> *Kick her in the guts, slam her in the head,*
> *Jump on her bones till she's dead, dead, dead.*

I pretty much knocked that on the head. Brenda and the other girls had a much more suitable offering. Ann played the piano and the girls sang to 'The Brady Bunch' tune.

> *Here's the story of a selfish Princess*
> *Who is mean and only thinks about herself.*
> *She's so awful and so nasty*
> *And that is why she's been left on the shelf.*
> *All the people want to change her,*
> *She makes their life a misery,*
> *How they do it, is our story,*
> *So you'll just have to wait and see.*

Not bad for a start. Doesn't quite scan but, it is, after all, their project. Got a few more pages of the script done.

QUEEN: Call the court jester back again.

(*Court jester comes back in, with his clothes torn from the flogging.*)

QUEEN: We have to do something about the Princess, Mr Court Jester. Otherwise she will have us all hung, drawn and quartered and there'll be no one left in the kingdom.

COURT JESTER: Why should I help the Princess? She's only been mean to me. Had me flogged ten times for telling bad jokes, boiled in oil for daring to suggest she has no sense of humour, and when I dared to complain about my punishments, she put a funnel-web spider up my arse.

A and S again. The way their minds work is totally beyond me. They seem to be capable of the most appalling thoughts. Who is teaching them all this? (Their slag mothers no doubt – pick it up at the gym when they're not shagging the instructors.) I think they have a touch of Tourette's, quite frankly.

QUEEN: Mr Court Jester, I know our daughter has been mean to you, but you are our only hope. Please try and think of something.

(*Queen and courtiers leave. The Court Jester shakes his balls.*)

Think that should be 'bells', A and S again.

(*A trumpet sounds and all the people in the village are summonsed.*)

COURT JESTER: Come one, come all. The Queen needs our help.

(*People gather around.*)

COURT JESTER: Citizens, the Queen has asked for our help to change the Princess's wicked ways. Has anyone got any ideas?

PEOPLE: Kill the bitch. Smash her head in.

'Right,' I said, 'we need to know where the panto is going, otherwise we don't have a show. There's no point in having a good first act without a good climax.' The second act is always the hardest, I told them, but in this case, being a panto, the heroine should probably live happily ever after.

Bit of sniggering from Amanda and Sheridan, which was to be expected. 'But she's a bitch,' they said. 'A selfish bitch.'

I suggested that people can change. That when shown the error of their ways, they could go on to bigger and better things. Leap ahead in all sorts of creative and exciting ways.

'But what if she doesn't see the error of her ways?' they cried.

'Well then, she is doomed,' I said. 'Then we have a major tragedy on our hands – and we wouldn't want that now, would we?' I suggested that perhaps they could get together over the holidays and work on the second act – at least come up with some ideas. It was, after all, their idea to write a show.

Naturally Amanda and Sheridan pooh-poohed that. Why should they do any work over the holidays? They were going skiing with their parents. The others said they would try and organise some time together. So we left it at that. I hope they come up with something even remotely intelligent, but I have a bad feeling about this. I suggested that we meet at Monday lunchtime, first day back.

Disaster leaving school. I saw the Odd Job Man raking leaves in the car park, so to avoid him I took the path near the privet hedge. I crouched over with my head down and scurried along so he wouldn't see me. Unfortunately I slammed my face straight into Miss McConnichy's butt, nearly knocking her over. (Lucky I didn't disappear up her fundament is my reading of the situation, but I didn't think that was a wise thing to say at this point. God only knows what I would have found up there . . . a Roman legion?)

She was mortified by this rearguard attack. What did I think I was doing? I told her I was practising to be the back half of a donkey in a parade. She looked at me like I was a dung beetle. I ran to the car. The Odd Job Man had seen it all. He was pissing himself laughing.

Friday

Oh glory hallelujah. Thank god for the holidays. I couldn't have stood another day of St Augustine's. Time to rest and recuperate. Time to put my house in order, read my diary, sort out my life. Rang Alison to see if she might cut her holiday short, but I only got to speak to the answer-phone.

Had drinks with Ann after work. I was tempted to ask if she could teach me some lesbotic stuff, because I have really had it with men. I mean, how hard could it be if you just strapped on a dildo? As long as you didn't have to touch any girls' bits. Probably just as well I didn't. She asked me again whether I'd approached Jack yet. We needed to get on with the lighting plan. And who should turn up at the pub but guess who in his tight jeans and tee shirt? Ann called him over for a drink. I nearly gagged. I quickly told her not to mention the lighting. I would do that another time.

Mainly because I was thinking I could ask someone else. Not sure who, but anybody.

He came over with that stupid grin on his face, knowing damn well that I knew he'd seen me naked. Maybe he shagged me while I was passed out. Maybe he just slipped the head of his cock in for a moment or two, then left . . . though I would have woken up with a start, given the size of that member.

He offered to buy us a drink and I politely declined. He had the cheek to say, 'Good to see you're off the booze', so I ordered a vodka and tonic and downed it in one gulp. Then I ordered a double.

A while later, I must have got my heel caught on the bar railing because I was just in the middle of an amazing story when I fell off the barstool. Odd Job Man jumped in and caught me before I hit the floor. He took me out to Ann's car. She drove me home. It's as if he's point-scoring, just hanging about waiting to save me.

Anyway, Ann drove me home. She gave me a bit of a lecture, something about drinking too much, moving on, getting my arse into gear. She made some comment about my distinctly snobbish approach when it comes to people. That I should accept people for what they are and not prejudge them in any way. It's a pity Ann is a lesbian. We could be best friends. She seems to actually care about me. She then asked if I'd even bothered to thank Jack for looking after me, especially after I had vommied in his car. Oh brother. Is there anything else I did that I can't remember? Maybe I need to talk to Larry. See what he can remember. I'll invite him over tomorrow.

Saturday

'So, did he shag you and what was his cock like?' Larry screamed as soon as I opened the door.

'Huge,' I screamed back, pretending to be enthusiastic. 'Wrap your arms around it and weep.' The two of us fell about.

'And you thought it was a sock,' he reminded me. 'Remember? Just before you danced on the table top and showed your map of Tasmania . . .'

'Yes, yes,' I cut him short. I did not want to go there. 'Some things are best forgotten,' I said meaningfully. 'Would you mind opening the wine?'

But Larry just wanted to talk about the Odd Job Man. 'Are you sure he's not gay? I am totally in love with him. He's the most gorgeous man I have ever seen.'

Which surprised me. I mean, he does have a certain look, but that's where it ends. 'Not the way he shagged me,' I said, rolling my eyes.

'Tell me from the beginning,' he sighed. 'I want to know every delicious moment.'

Realised this was a splendid opportunity. If I laid it on thick enough, Larry would be bound to tell all to Jamie and then of course jealousy would spew from Jamie's heart and he would rush back to me. 'Well,' I said, 'as you know, I was a tad drunk. I tried to get out of the car. Jack told me to stay where I was, not to move. He came around to the side of the car, opened the door . . .'

Larry's head started to move slightly to one side in that gooey, luvvy sort of way that dogs do when they're sniffing another dog's butt. I decided to go all out. 'Jack leaned into the car with his strong muscular arms, his lips accidentally brushing my mouth. As if I was a feather, he picked me up and carried me towards the house. He kicked open the front gate, smashing it off its hinges . . .'

'I could feel his arousal,' I told Larry, 'a hardness like I'd never felt before, like a large hammer, and I knew at that moment I was going to be his anvil.' Larry crossed his legs at this point and his hand slipped nonchalantly into his pocket. Mind you, I was a little moist between the thighs myself. I went on: 'Jack carried me down the passageway, his stubble just grazing my chin. He laid me gently on the bed.

'He had turned to go,' I said huskily, 'when I called out to him. "Jack," I said, "Jack, don't go. Stay with me, make love to me," I begged. "Thrust your manliness into my body."

'I watched him undo the buckle on his belt, undo the zip and slowly ease his tight, tight leathers down over his manliness, revealing it for all to behold . . .' Drip drip drip went Larry. 'Well,' I said, 'Jack started to kiss me, everywhere, his genitals brushing over my body as he did so, his tongue searching my mouth, flicking here and there, then moving down my body till I was screaming out "Fuck me, fuck me." And then he entered me,' I told the totally enraptured Larry, 'but it was difficult because of the size of his member . . .'

I think it was at this point that Larry came. He pretended to lean over and retie his shoelaces, but there was a bit of shuddering and shaking going on. Mind you, I think I might have come a bit myself. Started throbbing between the legs. I've heard about mental orgasms – maybe this was one of them.

'So what happened next?' said Larry. 'Is there more?'

Now that I think about it, I probably went a bit far here, but if the message was to get back to Jamie, I had to do something. 'Oh yes,' I said, 'there's a lot more to the story.'

Larry sat on the edge of the chair. 'Do tell,' he said.

'After we made love and were lying there sated in our passion,' I lied, 'Jack told me he loved me. He said from day one, the first moment he had seen me, he knew he was deeply in love. I confessed that I loved him in return. He then asked me to marry him. He's out buying the engagement ring as we speak – Tiffany claw, two carat diamond.'

At this Larry was a bit taken aback, I could see. Was he going to fall for it? But Larry is a romantic, after all. Suddenly, tears rolled down his cheeks. 'That's the most beautiful love story I ever heard,' he sniffed. 'I am soooo happy for you, Maggs,' and he gave me a huge hug and a kiss. 'You have turned a corner, girlfriend.'

I stared at him. 'What sort of a corner?' I said.

Larry hesitated a little. 'All I'm saying is that it's good that you've fallen for a guy who's well . . . a janitor. It shows that you've accepted him for what he is.'

Maybe I should have shut up at this point, but I figured that if it got back to Jamie that I had fallen in love with a man who empties garbage, I would be a laughing stock. 'Well,' I said, 'funny you should mention it, but the fact is, he isn't really a janitor at all.' I was thinking on my feet, remembering something I'd read in one of Mum's romantic novels. 'He's actually the son of a wealthy industrialist.' Larry was looking at me quizzically, but I managed to keep going. 'His father wanted Jack to take on the family business . . . you know, woollen mills, oil fields, gold mines . . .'

'Do they have gold in Ireland?' he asked.

'Congo,' I said. 'In the Congo.' He seemed to buy that so I went on: 'Anyway, Jack decided to take a sabbatical, go see the world, see how the other half lives. He's not into money and wealth,' I said. 'He saw the ad for the job at the school and decided to apply. As he says, someone has to empty the bins of the world.' This I did with an Irish accent, which I think really helped my gambit.

Larry was impressed. 'Really?' he said. 'So he's a nice guy

as well as having a huge dick.' He got very emotional and his eyes filled with tears again. 'I'm just soooo pleased for you, Maggs. This is wonderful. I'm soooo glad you're happy.' He picked me up and swung me around with joy. I felt a bit awful then, seeing I'd told a huge porky.

'I'll tell you the truth,' he said. 'I never thought you and Jamie were meant for each other in the first place. I'm surprised it lasted as long as it did.'

I stared at him. 'Pardon?' I said, almost choking on my wine.

'Well, you always wanted him to be something he wasn't.'

I was staggered. 'What are you talking about?' I said.

'All that crap about him being a great writer,' he said. 'He was born for the public service.'

My lips started to purse at that stage. 'He is a great writer,' I said. 'He has talent. The way he put words together was amazing. All those poems he wrote.'

Larry paused for a moment. 'I wrote them,' he finally said.

I stared at him.

'Jamie was trying to live up to the image you had of him.'

'You wrote the poems?'

He nodded. I was lost for words. 'Your lips are like the sunlight falling on sheaves of wheat.' I stared at him. 'It was crap, Maggs. Don't know how you fell for it. Maybe you just wanted to.' My bottom lip was quivering by this stage. I bit it. 'But now you've met someone you really love, I can tell you this.'

I was stunned. Lost for words. Not sure why Larry would make up such a story. The quiche was burning. I made my escape and dried my tears.

Over dinner I diverted the conversation away from me and asked him about his boyfriend – which turned out to be a huge mistake, because he talked about him ad nauseum all night. I nodded a lot and pretended to be interested. Why do people talk about themselves all the time? Don't they know how annoying it is? Anyway, his boyfriend is coming out at the end of the month, a few weeks before Jamie's wedding. Turns out he's really in love (even though he shagged someone else at the party, which I didn't point out).

I gushed a lot and said how happy I was for him, although I found it all really tedious. Larry then got very excited. 'We'll have a dinner for four,' he said.

At this point I lost the plot a bit. 'Oh yes. You and Frederic and me and Jamie. It'll be fabulous.'

'Not Jamie,' he said. 'Jack.'

'Just a slip of the tongue,' I said. 'Jamie, Jack – two Js.' Think I got away with it. 'I accept on his behalf,' I said grandly.

'Oh, and you'll have the ring by then,' said Larry. 'I'm just dyyyyying to see it.'

Poop. I'll have to make something up and get out of that one. I have four weeks. Hopefully he'll have forgotten about it by then.

Got some info about the wedding. Larry is doing all the organising, from the buck's night to the honeymoon. That's his forte – organising – I think it's a gay thing. Said he was thinking about someone coming out of a cake for the buck's night. He'd seen it done in the States and it was a hoot. Thought Jamie would find it amusing. Not sure that he would, but didn't mention it. Larry is really a sweet guy. What a pity he's gay.

After he left I finished off all the wine.

Sunday

Went to Mum and Dad's. Sister, brother-in-law, kids there again. Mum asked if I was getting enough sleep. Brother-in-law said I looked like I'd been dragged through a chiko roll. I said he had a head like a rotating mallee root. We continued to hurl insults at each other until my sister screamed out, 'For god's sake, shut up!' I mean, how has she put up with such a puerile mind all these years? Does he think he's clever or something?

Then the kids rushed in. They love their Aunty Marg. When they realised I didn't have any lollies, they pissed off again. Kids. Maybe I should have kids. I'm good with them. Maybe that's what's missing in my life. Could that be what Alison was trying to say? You are the most earth motherly person I've ever known? Mind you, I was glad to see the back of them by early afternoon.

Lunch consisted of corned topside with cabbage and potato mash piled up like Mount Vesuvius. I was expecting it to erupt any minute. I was tempted to talk to Mum about 'presentation', but I think it's a lost cause. The gas heater blew up, which provided some light entertainment. Dad then related the story of his brother Wally who lit a match to see how much petrol he had left in the petrol tank. I wonder if madness is a family trait?

My sister drew me aside and started asking some weird questions, like was I eating properly, and how much was I drinking. No idea what she was on about. I said I'd never been better. She suggested I might like to use their on-site caravan up the coast during the school holidays. It might be a nice break. I said I'd let her know. Jamie and I had been there once and had a wonderful time. We walked along the sand arm in arm, we saw killer whales thrashing around with a half-eaten seal, we ate prawns and crayfish, drank wine, made love . . . Not sure I could face it on my own.

Mum got stuck into her Mills and Boons after lunch, the fag hanging out of her mouth. I slipped one up my jumper before I left. What a crock. This stuff has nothing to do with real life. People falling in love, living happily ever after. IT JUST DOESN'T HAPPEN. And why would Mum be reading them now? It's far too late for her. She must be over fifty. Mind you, she had something distinctly hickey-like on her neck the other week. Surely not? Need a drink. Got a bit left in the bladder – just needs a squeeze.

Gas fire going. It's cold today. And cold in my heart. At least I have two weeks of wonderful holidays stretching out before me. I can concentrate on myself, work on my plan to stop the wedding, study the baffling conundrum re 'you are the most . . .', maybe visit the art gallery, the museum, go to the movies, the zoo . . . I'm excited now. It will be an uplifting experience to get my mind active again. Maybe at the end of my R&R all my problems will be solved and I can give Alison the boot.

Monday

Went to the cinema. Wog movie with subtitles. Boring. No plan yet re sabotaging the wedding.

Tuesday

Went to the art gallery. Boring. No plan yet. Rang Alison. Still just the answer-phone. What is wrong with that woman?

Wednesday

Went to the zoo. Highlight of the day was two giraffes shagging each other.

Thursday

Went to the museum. Boring. All that dead crap. And still no clue about how to stop the wedding. Thought my brain would be stimulated by so much cultural activity. I am going mental.

Friday

Beginning to wonder about the nature of friendship. What does it mean in the scheme of things, exactly? I would have thought there was a certain amount of loyalty involved, a sharing-stroke-caring sort of arrangement, protecting each other from disaster or impending doom. That was what Gallipoli was all about, wasn't it? Mateship. So what sort of a friend is Dana, really? What sort of a friend would drop around and pretend to ask about your holidays, and then 'oh by the way', wave a wedding invitation in your face – an invitation to the nuptials of the man you love with some gutter creature – and not notice the pain and anguish it caused? I really need to question Dana's commitment here. Because if the shoe was on the other foot and a friend of mine needed thoughtfulness, tact, consideration, I would be there for them, I'm sure.

The invitation itself was tasteless and gaudy. I mean, anyone who thinks a rolled-up, wax-sealed invite hand-written in Olde English on parchment is (a) original or

(b) interesting shows an unbelievable lack of imagination. Surely Jamie would have seen by this display of boringness that to marry this girl is a travesty? Apparently the wedding invitations were delivered by a man dressed up in some sort of medieval cossie on a horse. I mean, who needs horse crap all over the street?

Dana then expressed her somewhat humble surprise that she had been invited at all as she'd only just met Lorelei. I suggested that if she'd sucked up Lorelei's arse any harder she would have had to call her 'Mother'. Dana feigned horror and said she found my attitude bitter and resentful. She thought it was time I embraced the situation with a full heart and open mind, that it was time to move on blah, blah, blah, and could she borrow my spotty dress, which she has always coveted, as she was a bit broke and didn't have anything to wear to the wedding. And what about the matching hat? Dana is a very cheap, shallow person, I have decided.

I smiled magnanimously and said of course she could and then pretended to be interested in the invitation. Dana handed it over. There it was in nauseating gold: Mrs Dickhead proudly announces the wedding of her daughter Slutface to Jamie, my own true love. It was too cruel to bear. But I quickly noted the details. Saturday 27 November, 11 am, St Aloysius Church and afterwards at Wentworth House. I was horrified. 'But he's not even Catholic,' I said. 'He's a total atheist. What the fuck is he doing?'

'He's taking instruction,' said Dana.

Right. That's it. I mean, all his values are going out the window. I can't let that happen. I have exactly eight weeks and one day to put my plan into action. If I had a plan, that is. Think. Think think . . . I have to stop the wedding at all costs. I am not thinking of myself here. I am thinking of Jamie being saddled with that tramp for the rest of his life. No, this will not do. I need to act now. But how?

2 am. Finished the cask. Still no plans.

Saturday

Have just driven past the church where the nuptials are to be held. An interesting grassy knoll on one side, an abandoned warehouse on the other. One could get in two clear shots... what am I talking about? I'm not going to prison for those losers. There has to be something else.

I need to point out to Jamie the obvious mistake he is making with his choice of partner. It is clear to me now that he felt sorry for Lorelei because of her father's demise, and was marrying her out of pity, and I wouldn't be the good friend I am if I didn't tell him that. I would sit him down and pose certain questions to him, like: are you really being fair to Lorelei? How is it possible to love someone else so quickly, particularly after the deep and meaningful relationship we had? You are obviously on the rebound, I would hate to see Lorelei hurt, it's not too late to call off the wedding, I know we've had our differences but I'm sure we could work things out... My plan was to give him food for thought in a calm, reasonable, intelligent way. Common sense, a rational discussion. I feel the need to put across my point of view. I need to act now.

Events didn't go exactly as planned. When I arrived at Jamie's, Lorelei's pale blue Audi sports car was parked in the driveway. I stood staring at it, then started to have some sort of attack. Something welled up in me, a sort of primal, lizard-brain thing erupted as if from a prehistoric past. It was do or die. Fight or flight. I was Neanderthal woman standing in front of the sabre-toothed tiger. I lost all control.

I opened my bag and took out my Purple Passion lipstick. As if some mysterious force was guiding my hand I started to write obscenities all over the car. I was halfway through a large 'cunt' on the windscreen when I tripped over the rock border on the driveway. I stubbed my toe and let out an almighty yell. The front light went on and Lorelei and Jamie came to the door. I hopped up the street, jumped into my car and took off. Not sure whether they saw me. I drove off like a madwoman, then realised I could be in big trouble.

4 am and am now sitting in my sister's caravan in terrible pain with my toenail turning black. Needed an alibi. Drove home, grabbed some clothes and my diary, and drove like crazy up the coast. After four hours on the highway, a terrible storm broke. Wind, rain, hail. I couldn't see a thing. It's god's punishment, I thought, except I don't believe in that shit. Another couple of hours further on, the storm was worse. The caravan is rocking now. The wind is howling and the rain pelting down. Thunder and lightning crashing all around. And I am stuck now in this godforsaken hole, possibly for the rest of the week.

Tried to ring Dana on my mobile to let her know where I was re the alibi, but the mobile is out of range. No power in the caravan. Couldn't find all the stuff in the dark. No gas or water either. Have a candle going. Only my trusty cask to keep me warm. It is fucking freezing.

Sunday

Hardly slept a wink. Storm has not abated. Heard on the radio that gale force winds have blown all the fishing boats onto the rocks. People missing, feared drowned. And more to the point, what am I going to have for breakfast? Have to go to the shops, maybe get some eggs and bacon. Need to turn the power, gas and water on. Number one priority is to ring Dana and let her know where I am. Public phone box at the shops.

The first thing she said was, 'They know it's you and Lorelei's thinking of taking out a restraining order.'

I pretended I had no idea what she was talking about. 'Sorry, what's that?' I said innocently.

'The stuff you wrote all over Lorelei's car. You are totally weird.'

'Hang on,' I said, 'I have to put some more coins in the phone. No reception on the mobile. At my sister's caravan up the coast. Left just after I saw you.'

'Is that your alibi, is it?' she said. 'You are such a bullshit artist. How come you didn't mention it when I saw you?'

'Well, it was just a spur of the moment decision,' I said. Now I really winged it: 'A . . . friend,' I said, 'thought it might be quite romantic to have a week together in an isolated place. Just the two of us.'

Dana took the bait. 'The two of who?' she said. 'Who are you talking about?'

'Just someone,' I said. 'Can't tell you who, all I can say is I'm having the time of my life.'

Luckily the coins ran out at that point.

Have managed to get the power and the gas on, but the water is another story. There is a pole with several water connections attached for the various caravans. Instructions are that you turn on the tap in the caravan, go to the pole, turn the connection on, then run back to the caravan which is a couple of blocks away, and if the water is running in the sink it's the right one. Except they are not named or numbered.

Have tried every fucking connection, can't seem to find the right one. I need help here. Trouble is, there is no one around. I am the only person, it seems, in the whole caravan park. After trying all the water connections several times, I have given up. It means I will have to haul water from the tap and use the public showers. Great. All that icky stuff on the floor. And the toilet in the caravan isn't working either. Will have to sit on public seats. Could catch anything.

So now what? Have bought a few supplies. Some bread, sausages, baked beans, couple of bottles of wine. Seafood shop closed due to the weather. Apparently their fisherman is one of those lost at sea. Damn. I was looking forward to some local prawns.

Rain still belting down. Bought some magazines which I read. Load of crap, really. 'Did Becks really shove it up his PA?' Don't know who reads them.

Now what? Lunch, I suppose. Sausages could be just a tad off. I guess with no one being here, the turnover is pretty poor. Will go up later to the local pub for dinner. Could be very inspiring. Hear jolly stories of whales and adventures. An old fisherman, maybe, singing a sea shanty. These coastal towns are full of atmosphere . . .

Four people at the pub, all watching football on TV. An old drunk made a pass at me. I was almost tempted. Am so horny. Back in the caravan now. Only eight thirty. This is pitiful. How many days do I have to stay here?

Monday

Had a terrible nightmare. I was walking down the aisle in a beautiful white dress. Sound of a choir singing, Dad at my side. Page boys, bridesmaids, the church was packed. Jamie was standing at the altar, but when he turned around to greet me it was the Odd Job Man. Woke up in a sweat.

Rain eased slightly. Went for a walk on the beach. Lots of debris washed up on the shore. I related to that. I am just a part of the flotsam and jetsam of the world.

Tuesday

Raining again. Thunder, lightning. Not sure I can hack another day of this wasteland. Rang Alison on the public phone. Still not answering. Left a message saying that I was getting myself together at the beach. Will spend the rest of the day going through my diary, see if I can find a clue to what Alison is on about.

No clues, no plan, no nothing. I am up the proverbial creek. I am so lonely I could die. Baked beans for dinner and a bottle of red. Pathetic. Problem is, if I go back too soon, it will look as if I've told a giant porky.

Sound of a car pulling up at the next caravan. Yippee. Friends of my sister's, Patty and Graeme. Nice people. They like me a lot. I'll grab a bottle of wine and go over. Company at last. Oh joy. Be able to play cards, tell stories, haven't seen them for years. They will be so surprised . . .

Shit. Was about to take a bottle next door when I heard loud yelling and cries of angst. Thought it might have been a domestic but as I went closer I heard Patty crying. Somebody had turned the water connection on at the pole and their caravan was completely flooded. Their holiday was ruined.

Thought it would be better if I quietly slipped away into the night. Have just arrived home.

Wednesday

Trapped in my house. Decided to clean out the fluff from under the bed. Got stuck. The neighbour's cat came in and licked my nose. I thought he was so cute. Then he turned his butt around and sprayed my face. I'll kill the little fucker. Sat on the verandah steps smoking and drinking for the rest of the day, trying to come up with a plan re getting Jamie back. Feel like shit. Bored, bored, bored out of my fucking brain.

Thursday

Still trapped in the house. Running out of food. Rang Alison yet again. Still the answer-phone. What is going on? I mean, fits are over in a minute. You put the furniture back in place, you mend the broken stuff and you forget all about it. That's what I've been led to believe. It's not like you have them for days. I'm inclined to think Alison is a malingerer.

Better study my diary, keep looking for that clue. 'You are the most . . . you are the most' . . . what Alison? Maybe the thesaurus would help. I'll just open a new cask first. You are the most . . . marvellous, astonishing, astounding, spectacular . . .

Bit pissed now . . .

Friday

Rang Dana, told her I was just back.

'Really?' she said. 'I saw the light on Wednesday night. What have you been doing? Hiding under the bed?'

I didn't bother to reply. Asked her what was happening re the AVO. She said she hadn't heard, but Lorelei was furious about her new car being damaged. I reminded Dana that they had no proof and that I was away at the time, and what a wonderful time I had had . . . I'm not sure whether she bought the story. But I think I am free and clear re the damage to the car.

Saturday

Message on my answer-phone from Jamie. Oh joy. Oh breath of spring. He has realised his mistake. Have a small drink, savour the moment. Make the call now.

Unbelievable. Jamie has taken the slut's side. What the fuck is going on here? Lorelei wants me to pay for the damage to her car. The bill was $2000. The dye from the lipstick had apparently ruined the duco. Incredible. And more to the point, what damage has it done to my lips?

I told Jamie I would love to have done it, but it wasn't me. For some reason he didn't believe me. He suggested it might be a nice gesture if I paid. Lorelei is really upset. 'It's not the money,' he said, 'but the principle.' Then he hung up.

What principle? What fucking principle? Here is some woman with more money than you can poke a stick at wanting compensation for her stupid car. This slut who stole my boyfriend without a by-your-leave. And she's daring to talk about principle? In a fucking pig's eye. Why is Jamie being so horrible to me?

Cat from next door in. He is sitting staring at me. At least he's not spraying. So far.

Sunday

Must have drunk half a cask of that dreadful wine last night. Hangover.

Went to Mum and Dad's. Mum cooked a dish she called Help Yourself – a sort of self-styled bolognese. Not sure it had anything to do with the cuisine of Italy, but there was some spaghetti floating in it, so I gave it the benefit of the doubt. The sauce had started life as some sort of animal, I assume, something that had obviously been driven across the Nullarbor during the drought and died on the way. I suggested that if she had sealed the meat in the frying pan with garlic and oil, maybe oregano or basil, before it went into the pot, it may have retained more of its flavour and been a little more palatable.

Mum, however, was of the opinion that you can't be too careful nowadays, what with Mad Cow disease and hydatids lurking everywhere, and boiling the meat was a sure-fire way to kill everything. I was about to explain that there was no Mad Cow disease in Australia and the meat was inspected for tapeworm, but Mum wasn't listening. In fact the point of the dish was that when it was launched en masse into a large bowl, everyone could 'help themselves' hence the name of the dish. Mum very proud of herself. Couldn't argue with that logic.

After 'helping myself' to a small amount of lunch I suddenly had a flash. Of course! The wise old man. In every great epic tale there is a 'wise old man', someone who knows the truth about everything and enlightens the protagonist along the way with words of wisdom. Shakespeare's fool, Tiresias the blind soothsayer in Greek mythology, Obi-wan Kenobi in *Star Wars* – or was it that rubber puppet? Can't remember. Anyway, my dad. Why didn't I think of it before?

Dad is amazingly perceptive in so many ways. He knew I was shoplifting when I was fourteen – mind you, I was wearing Gucci and Christian Dior on a very small amount of pocket money, so it probably wasn't a major leap. He predicted that I would not make a good teacher . . . well, I've proved him wrong on that score, but in most things he is spot-on. Anyway, Dad would set me on the path to reunification.

He was out in the shed making his home brew. There is always something mystical about Dad's shed . . . the smell of glue lingering from the old days when he used to mend our shoes, the bits and pieces hanging from the roof, the old hedge clippers, old lawnmower parts, my old bicycle in the corner, rusty and full of cobwebs (a life well lived), jars of nails, screws, tools of every description hanging on the walls. A magical place and just the setting, I thought, to get the answer to my conundrum.

Decided not to tell him re shrink. Didn't want him to think I needed that kind of help. So I put it to him like this: 'Dad,' I said, 'if someone asked you to describe me in one sentence, say, "You are the most something something something something", what would you say?'

'Been seeing a shrink, have you?' said Dad, writing in his beer logbook. 'Trying to sort out your life?' He is totally amazing . . . He paused for a moment or two. I noticed the sun shining in through the window, the gentle bubbling of the hops on the small gas stove – the perfect place to do some problem-solving. 'Let's see,' he pondered. 'What about you are the most selfish, self-centred, egocentric, self-absorbed, pompous, conceited, stuck-up snob I've ever known?'

My dad is a very funny man. He cracks me up. And so perceptive. He could obviously see that I was a bit down and just wanted to make me laugh. Our little conversation cheered me up no end.

School tomorrow. And still no plan in place for fucking up Jamie's wedding and sending him back to me where he belongs. Can't believe my holidays have been such a waste of time. And now I'm faced with another endless cycle of pure torture. Hope the nerds have come up with an idea for the panto.

Monday

I knew this would happen, I just knew it. As if I haven't got enough on my plate. I knew that when the drama girls suggested they write their own material, I would end up doing it. Two weeks they had, two weeks to come up with a second act for the panto, and not one idea was forthcoming at our lunchtime meeting. Zilch. Well, discounting some lewd suggestions from Amanda and Sheridan. If it wasn't for my tenuous position at the school, I would cancel the panto, explain to Miss McConnichy that the feeble brains in the drama group have been unable to rub two ideas together. I mean, how hard could it be? I will now have to think of something before Thursday. As if I have time to waste on this shit. But my future might depend on my success.

Tuesday

Rang Alison and left a message. Told her if she wasn't back on deck soon, I'd have to get another shrink. I need help here.

Message from Alison on my answer-phone when I got home. She gave me a few names and contact details for other shrinks. What is she trying to do? Get rid of me? Is that what the problem has been all along? She has no idea how to handle me. This is not my fault at all. Shrinks aren't supposed to like their patients. They're supposed to help them.

Left another message, and this time I sucked a bit. Said she was the best shrink in the world and I was really sorry I'd mentioned the hirsute upper lip. Haven't heard back.

Wednesday

It's now all-out war with the Odd Job Man. First he was in my parking space again, then there was the whipper-snipper around my legs as I ate lunch on the front lawn, then he was outside the window again, cleaning the down-pipes, pressing his genitalia onto the glass. What is he trying to prove? I need to report him to someone, but I feel all my avenues are closed. He is harassing me. Next he'll be stalking me, ringing me up at all hours of the night, driving past my house. The man is totally off his nut.

Shit. Have to come up with panto plot by tomorrow. How hard can it be? How can we punish the princess? Maybe need a drink to get my brain going.

Midnight: have come up with the panto plot. I think it is brilliant.

Thursday

Pitched the second act to the drama club. The villagers decide to hire a handsome young swineherd who is an amazing rake and lover in the town. He has magical powers when it comes to women. Everyone who sees him falls in love with him.

'Does he have a big cock?' said Amanda.

I ignored her and went on. They dress him up as a prince and he woos the princess, who falls head over heels in love with him. He then reveals his true identity. Her heart is dashed to pieces. She will be knocked off her pedestal and humiliated for loving someone of such lowly birth. She will become the laughing stock of the kingdom and will be despised by all and sundry.

For once Amanda and Sheridan thought it was a great idea, although they still wanted the princess to 'top' herself. The other girls, however, were not happy. There was dissent in the ranks. Brenda led the charge. 'But, Miss,' she said, 'where is the sea change? You said that the princess needed to see the error of her ways. What is the moral here? She's been humiliated. She hasn't changed at all. There is no growth in the character.'

Shit. Why did I tell them all that rubbish? At least I suppose it proves some of them were listening. But Brenda was on a roll now. 'And where is the happy ending? We don't want to put a negative spin on life for the littlies, surely.'

I was stunned. 'All right,' I said, my lips pursing, 'you tell me a better ending, Brenda, and I will be quite happy to consider it.' I mean, what a cheek. I had spent all night coming up with that scenario and now some fat girl was challenging it.

'Okay,' said Brenda, 'why doesn't she get to know the

swineherd better and find all these wonderful qualities in his character that far outweigh the fact that he is poor and of lowly birth? And along the way, he brings out the goodness and niceness in the princess and they both fall in love and live happily ever after.'

'And do they go and live in the swineherd's house? The princess in all her finery feeding the pigs?' I said, with just a hint of sarcasm.

'Well, it doesn't really matter,' said Brenda, 'if they love each other.'

The other girls applauded, except of course for A and S, who at least were on my side. I suggested we take a vote on it but the fat girl and friends had the numbers.

Ann arrived at the end of it all and thought it was a great idea. I was pissed off, but hid it. Didn't want them to think I was precious about my idea. I was magnanimous. 'Fine,' I said, 'let's go with it.'

So the girls started writing feverishly. Except Amanda and Sheridan, who said they had to go to the toilet urgently. No doubt going out for a smoke, but I knew their contribution to the script would be minimal and I was glad to get rid of them.

Am I suffering with early-onset Alzheimer's? Took my diary to school to continue the search for the missing link that will unlock the 'you are the most' conundrum. Major panic. Thought I'd misplaced it there for about half an hour during drama. Turned the place upside down. As it turned out it was in my basket all the time. Maybe I shouldn't bring it to school, but it gives me the opportunity to peruse it in my spare periods. This is the joy of being a drama teacher: very little preparation – you just wing it on the day.

Friday

Kids talking about the Halloween disco in a couple of weeks. Much excitement. Everyone discussing their costumes. Witches seem to be the most popular, with a few ghosts and some skeletons. Sheridan and Amanda were unusually quiet. I asked them if their costumes were a secret. For a moment they didn't say much, just looked at each other. Then Sheridan said tightly, 'In case you've forgotten, Miss, we're grounded for the rest of the year. We're not allowed to go.'

I felt a little sorry for them. Hope they're not still blaming that on me.

Alison rang, left another message. Why she always rings at home when she knows I'm at school is beyond me. At least she's communicating again. Means she's getting better. Anyway, she has suggested that before we resume any counselling, I need to sit down and think about where I am at — what my current state of mind is, what my feelings are. Try and delve deep inside and think about what is going on. She can then assess if we have made any progress at all.

What is this? Homework? That's what I was paying her to do, to work this shit out for me. I'll see if I have time over the weekend.

Saturday

Right. Done the vacuuming, shopping, the washing. What is it Alison wants me to look at? Ah here it is . . . blah blah blah, look deep down, see if I've progressed blah blah and search for the answer to you are the most . . . It's in your diary. How does she know? She hasn't read it. Look for an emerging pattern. Right. Well, yes, I can see something here. I am obviously the victim of a cruel plot . . . people are out to get me. Jamie leaving me for no apparent reason, Lorelei stealing my man, Dana my best friend sucking up to the aforementioned, the Odd Job Man harassing me . . . Amanda and Sheridan hating my guts, my brother-in-law ditto, the cat (well, I suppose it can't really be included), and let's not forget dear old Alison herself. It's all starting to fall into place. A conspiracy. I'll ring Alison, tell her what I have come up with, see if that makes her happy.

Alison answered the phone. She was expecting a call from some doctor. Her mother is dying or something. Said I would only keep her a minute or two. Threw the conspiracy theory at her. She hung up. What is *wrong* with that woman?

   I'm bored now, trying to sort this out. I'll ring Dana, see what she's doing.

This is unbelievable. Dana is going over to the Rhine slut's place for dinner. I could hardly contain my anger. So what's left for me this Saturday night? A video and a cask, I suppose. Too late to ring anyone to ask them over. Maybe I should go to the movies . . . although going to the movies on your own on a Saturday night is pretty sad. Maybe I should go to a bar and pick up someone . . . not sure I could hack vaginal warts again. Cask and video sounding okay. Cat from next door in again. Miaowing away. Just jumped up on my lap. Wants to be friendly this time. He's quite cute in a weird sort of way.

He did it again. Little pussy bastard. Have to get the cloth. What is going on in my life when even a stray cat wants to spray in my face? The universe is out to get me. Why? What have I done?

Sunday

Went to Mum and Dad's. Cold collations. Boiled mutton, chopped iceberg lettuce. Sliced orange and banana. Tomato, cucumber and onion with some dressing made from sweetened condensed milk. I was relieved. Not much can go wrong with a basic salad.

Some fantastic news. My Aunt Penelope, Mum's sister, is coming home. She's been lecturing in economics at the Sorbonne in Paris. She's amazing. I had always hoped secretly that she was my real mother. That I had been adopted by Mum and Dad while she pursued her career and that one day she would announce the truth. Maybe that's why she is visiting now. Then I could take my rightful place in the world as the daughter of an intellectual.

She never married – not sure why. Maybe she had her heart broken along the way or something. Used to be a big hockey player as I recall – vice captain of the state team. Old friend of Miss McConnichy's. They were roommates at university – the only reason I got the job at St Augustine's. Haven't seen her for about five years. Mum is excited. She adores her sister. Mum is so dull by comparison. Funny how two members of the same family can be so different. A bit like my sister and I. We shared the same room for seventeen years before she married the nerd. I still don't know anything about her.

Monday

I am totally reeling with shock. Dana turned up after work. 'Guess what?' she said.

'The wedding's off,' I replied smugly. 'I knew it wouldn't last. They are soooo not suited.'

'I thought you were over him?' she said.

I laughed scornfully. 'Of course I'm over him. Well, is it off or not?'

'No, it's not off. One of Lorelei's bridesmaids is up the duff and she's asked me to fill in.'

'Fill in what?' I said.

'Her place, as one of the bridesmaids.'

'You said no of course.'

'Why would I do that?' she cried.

'Well, you hardly know Lorelei, for starters, and . . . what about me?' I whimpered.

'What about you what?' she said.

'You're supposed to be my best friend.'

'What's that got to do with anything?'

'What about my relationship with Jamie? You can't just ignore that.'

'What are you talking about?' she retorted. 'You don't have a relationship with Jamie anymore. He dumped you months ago and he's about to marry someone else.'

'But I'm still in mourning,' I said. 'There hasn't been a grieving time.'

'I can't help that,' she said. 'That's your problem, not mine. Besides, it's going to be the wedding of the year. It'll make all the social pages. Got to go now,' she said. 'We're having a wedding rehearsal at the church in half an hour. It's going to be so much fun.'

And with that she ran out the door. 'Oh,' she called back, 'I won't be needing your spotty dress or the hat. We'll be wearing Collette Dinnigan. Lorelei's mother is footing the bill and we're allowed to keep the frocks after.' And she was gone. I needed a drink.

Forcing myself to write now. Bit pissed. Am so alone. Doesn't anyone care how I feel? What sort of a friend would do such a thing? I have hit rock bottom. Think, girl, think. Need to open another bottle first.

Oh my god. What is happening in my life? I cannot believe what has happened. Decided it was time to act. Decided that I'd had enough. It was time to confront the situation. I was going to the church, to the rehearsal, to upset the apple cart. The perfect plan came to me as I was weaving along the freeway. It was all so clear, as though a veil had lifted from my eyes. I knew exactly how to shaft the wedding!

I would run into the rehearsal crying, 'Stop the proceedings, this wedding cannot take place!' They would all stare – all the stupid bridesmaids, flower girls and boys, the ushers, the assorted parents. They would stand stock still in the church, gaping at the distraught woman – me – sobbing in the aisle. I would drop to my knees, shaking in the silence. The late afternoon sun would drift in through the stained glass windows lighting up the fat baby infant sucking on the Virgin's bosom, or maybe the crucified Jesus with the blood dripping from the wound in the side, the nails (even though they never crucified with nails in those days) protruding from Jesus' hands and feet, the crowd fighting over the robe. Haloes of light around all the main players, Mary the mother, Mary the hooker, couple of disciples who would write the epistles forty years later and would somehow manage to remember all the finer details, except that some remembered details others didn't . . .

I would grab the chamois from the back of the car and tie it around my head to give me a certain waif-like humbleness. 'I'm pregnant,' I would say in hushed tones. 'I am carrying Jamie's child.'

At that moment, Jamie's mother would rush over, tears running down her face. She would touch my stomach and turn to her husband, Lou, who was always trying to put his hand up my skirt and making lewd suggestions to me. 'Lou,' she would say, 'it's our grandchild. Margaret is carrying our grandchild!' Then, turning to Jamie with a look of reproach, she would chastise him: 'How could you, Jamie, how could you do such a thing?'

Lorelei would scream, tearing her hair out and renting her clothes. She would now be revealed in all her true colours. She would say terrible things, possibly speak in tongues, lightning would flash, and she would curse Jamie, tell him that she was only marrying him out of spite and that his dick was too small, at which point Jamie would defend himself by saying that maybe it was her snatch, maybe her twat had been used so many times that it had stretched beyond belief and he was surprised her womb hadn't fallen out.

A punch-up would ensue and the two of them would be pulled apart. Jamie's mother would then hold her hands up for silence. A deathly hush would fall in that holiest of places. She would take her time to speak. 'We have organised the caterers, the presents have started to arrive, the dresses have been ordered and the cake has been iced with almond paste. It is too late. This wedding will take place.' She would slowly turn to look scornfully at the slut from the Rhine: 'Not with Lorelei, but with Margaret, who is carrying the heir to our estate. Margaret, who we always liked, who we were most happy with and always wanted for our daughter-in-law . . .' All this and more was in my mind as I drove to the church.

It was the perfect plan – except for one thing. Not the fact that I wasn't pregnant (I would later say I sadly miscarried) but the red light that I didn't see as I was approaching the church. And the man on the bicycle I didn't see crossing in front of me on the green light. Nor did I see the police car behind me, whose occupants witnessed the whole unfortunate scene. Luckily the man on the bicycle swerved to avoid a collision as I screeched to a halt. He screamed out, 'Cunt!' The police didn't take this abuse into consideration when they pulled me over.

The constable asked me whether I'd had a drink today. Stupidly said I couldn't remember. He then asked me to blow into the bag, just as the wedding party were coming out of the church. Oh humiliation beyond belief. The test, for some reason, indicated I was well over the legal limit.

'Get out of the car, girlie,' said the constable. 'You're coming with us. And hand over your licence. You won't be driving again for some time.' My protests re the unreliability of the test results went down the gurgler as I stumbled out of the car.

Dana spotted me being helped up by the two policemen. 'Oh look,' she announced to everyone, 'Margaret's been copped for drunk driving. Surprised she's gotten away with it for so long. She has a bit of a problem, you know. And what are you doing here anyway?' she called out to me. 'I thought you were over Jamie.'

'Is there anyone who can drive your car home?' asked the Constable. At that point I saw Jamie heading towards me – no doubt to comfort and reassure me. He would help me in my hour of need.

But no. 'Let this be a lesson to you Maggs,' he chided. 'It's a timely warning. You could have hit a child.'

'What about me, arsehole?' screamed the bike man, pretending there was something wrong with his knee.

Jamie blushed and apologised. 'No offence,' he said.

'Pig's arse,' said the man.

Lorelei came over, gave me a cute little smile and wave, and hooked her arm into Jamie's. 'Come on,' she said to him, 'we're due at Maxim's for supper,' and they all went skipping off.

Only Larry stayed. He volunteered to drive the car home and pick me up later from the police station. I was then stuffed into the paddy wagon.

Spent the next two hours in a cell at the local lock-up. My second reading had somehow sky rocketed. I complained again about their faulty equipment, but to no avail. I was charged with drunken driving and have to appear in court in a month. Can my life get any worse?

On the way home Larry asked me what I was going to do now. 'I have no idea,' I told him.

'Well, thank your lucky stars,' he said, trying to put a positive spin on the situation, 'that you didn't hit the man on the bike. It could have been a lot worse.'

'How much worse?' I sobbed. 'How much worse can one's life be?'

'At least you've got Jack,' he said kindly. 'Are you going to call him?'

'I don't want him to know,' I mumbled. We pulled up at my place.

'He'll find out sooner or later. No point in lying to the one you love.' He kissed me on the cheek and I stepped out of his car to go inside.

I'm glad I didn't vacuum under the bed. This fluff is soooo comforting. Cat came under with me. Didn't spray. He just licked my tears. I think he likes the salt.

Tuesday

Couldn't face school today. Besides, I would have had to get public transport. I can't stand public transport.

Rang Dad and asked if he could fix my bike. Told him I was on a 'get fit' mission. I was going to ride my bike to school every day.

'Lost your licence, did you?' he said. 'Drunk driving? Bound to happen one day,' he said.

Why does everyone think I have a drinking problem? I hate that. Can't they see that I'm deeply depressed and that drinking helps to clear my mind?

Larry put me onto a lawyer, Raymond. He says I will probably get a year's suspension and a fine. He suggested that I should maybe see a shrink, so that it will appear to the court that I am at least trying to solve my problems.

'But I don't have any problems,' I said.

'That's not the point,' he replied. 'It would just look better for the judge. And if you could get a couple of referees . . .'

Rang Alison (she actually answered the phone), blurted out what happened, begged her to see me. There was silence at the other end. She said if she had a cancellation she might see me next week. 'Next week? I need help now,' I shrieked.

'Have you solved the puzzle yet?' she added. 'Don't bother to come unless you have,' she said sweetly.

I'm sure she slammed the phone down. What *is* her problem? Maybe her husband has left her. At least that might give her an insight into how my life is barely hanging together.

Dad brought the bike over. He'd even given it a coat of paint. He is amazing, my dad. He is a real Mr Fix-it Man.

Wednesday

It's much further to school than I thought. Had a sore snatch by the time I arrived. It's a while since I've been on a bicycle seat. Arrived late. Miss McConnichy was with my class in the quadrangle. Trust her to find them. They were running amok. I told her I'd been in a serious accident yesterday and that my car had caught fire and as a result I'd had to ride my bike and then I'd had a flat tyre and had to change the wheel and then the brakes failed and I almost hit an old lady, so I had to sit and talk to her till she calmed down. Not sure whether she bought it or not. Maybe I shouldn't have embellished so much.

I could see she was about to tell me off, so I quickly changed the subject. Told her Aunt Penelope was coming home from overseas. Really odd look on Miss McConnichy's face. She nodded and walked off. Wonder what that was all about. Hope they're still friends or my job could be a pile of nanny goat's shit. Maybe they fought once, over a man.

Amanda and Sheridan said I must have had a good weekend, from the way I was walking. I ignored them. They are so cheap, those two. Gutter tramps. But I was surprised when, at the end of the class, they offered to carry my bag and books back to the staffroom, which was a huge relief. Only Amanda dropped them, of course. Was it deliberate? I think they're still pissed off with me for being grounded.

Ann said she would be my referee. I was grateful. Would it go against me if the court knew she was lesbian? Need another four referees. Do I have four friends?

Snatch getting sorer as the day goes on. Might have to walk home wheeling my bike. Great.

Thunderstorm. Rain bucketing down. Lightning flashing. Waiting in the staffroom until the storm abates. Everyone else gone for the day. Writing in my diary while I hang around. Oh shit. The Odd Job Man has just come in dragging his wheelie bin. I'll keep writing in here and pretend I haven't seen him.

Unbelievable. He is totally ignoring me. What is his problem? Maybe I should say something about him taking me home. But then I'll have to mention the undressing bit, apologise for throwing up in his car. Not sure I can open up the subject. Have to say something soon or there's no way he'll do the panto sets, and my one and only other hope, Barry Day, the science teacher said he was taking paternity leave. Bummer.

He's trying to attract my attention. What *is* his problem? I will ignore him. He is pointing to the bin. 'The bin under the desk,' he says. I move my legs sideways. He leans down, brushing my leg with the back of his hand as he reaches for the bin. I'm sure it was deliberate. He empties the bin.

'Taking to riding your bike, I see? Lose your licence for drunk driving?' The next person who says that, I am going to spew. I am not answering, I just keep writing.

'I have to fix the heating unit,' he says. 'If you don't mind hanging around, I could drive you home again.'

Why did he have to say *again*? It's the familiarity I can't bear. It's like we know each other or something. Then again, I was naked in the bed when I woke up, so he must know something about me. 'I'm fine,' I say without turning around. Lightning is flashing outside. Shit.

'Well,' he says, 'if you change your mind, let me know.'

Oh my god. What have I done? Is this some sort of a terrible dream? Oh please, let me wake up – please tell me it's all a gigantic nightmare. Please, please, please – how did I get myself into this situation?

Possibly my big mistake was to ignore the Odd Job Man. I could have forced out a quick thank-you on the spot re the taking home, then moved on to the sets and the lighting and sound for the panto – all within the safety of the staffroom. But I didn't. Was it pride? Or just plain stupidity? Now that I think about it, thank-yous are not really my forte. Thank and you are words that rarely come out of my mouth, at least not together. They make you beholden in some way, like you owe people.

After the Odd Job Man left the room, I did feel a bit guilty – after all, I had now finished a drawing of the set and a simple plan for the lighting grid in the hall, and I needed to get it finalised. Thought I could just quickly apologise, hand him the drawings and rush off.

There was no one around, except for the admin staff still in the office. I remembered that the heating unit was housed in the old boiler room around the side of the school. The weather had really closed in now, making the place quite dark and spooky. I got caught by a leaking downpipe, soaked me completely. I looked like a drowned rat, but I wasn't there to impress – only to manipulate the situation somehow. I could hear banging on pipes as I went down the sideway. There was a light coming from the boiler room, which was accessed by a flight of stairs down into what the students called the dungeon.

Down, down I went, heading for the light in the darkness. He looked up as I entered, spanner in hand. Then a strange thing happened. I was completely lost for words. I began to stutter, tongue-tied for some reason. 'Th-th-th,' I said, as if I had some terrible affliction.

The Odd Job Man sat and waited.

'Th-th-th,' I stammered.

'Yes?' he said. 'What is it you're trying to say?'

Suddenly it came out in a barely audible rush: 'Thanksfortheothernighttakingmehomewhen Iwasdrunkanddisorder lyandcouldyoudothesoundandthelightingforthepantoanddid youseemenaked?'

The Odd Job Man stared at me, a strange sort of smile on his face. 'Sorry?' he said. 'What was that?'

'Thanks for the other night and could you do the sound and lighting for the panto and did you see me naked?'

He began to laugh.

'What?' I bleated. 'Why are you laughing?'

'Because you are such a funny girl,' he said gently.

Suddenly, he moved in close to me, about two inches from my face. I could feel the heat from his body. It was as though I was frozen. I couldn't breathe. He then moved in, his lips just grazing mine. I could smell his breath. It was hot and musty. His tongue flicked momentarily into my mouth, then again, this time exploring, eating me, gently, then getting harder. I tried to resist, but found myself responding.

He said nothing as he unbuttoned my blouse. Why hadn't I worn a bra today? They were all in the wash, as I fleetingly recalled. So my bare breasts were now exposed. His eyes scorched mine as he ran his hands over my breasts, then his tongue, so light, so delicate. He was kissing me on the mouth again as his hand moved up under my skirt, his fingers searching between my legs.

I tried to protest. 'Stop, stop,' I cried. 'Please . . . please, you mustn't,' but it was too late. His fingers hooked under my panties, reaching into the waiting cavern. I was unmasked now as his digits plunged into the wetness they found. I was lost. I was in his power.

I reached out like a drowning person, only to brush

accidentally against the huge hardness beneath his overalls. He pushed my hand away and pinned me to the wall with brute force. He began to move down my body with his tongue, until he reached the last hidden crevice. I was now almost naked, my clothes torn asunder. In one deft movement, the Odd Job Man unbuttoned his overalls and entered me. Time stood still. He didn't move. His great cock just stayed there, pulsating in that hollow place –

At that precise moment, choir practice began in the chapel. They were singing 'Ave Maria' as the Odd Job Man gripped my buttocks and began slowly moving his large member in and out of my wetness. Suddenly I found myself moving with him. Was it the sound of the rain drumming on the roof? I'm sure it was just my innate sense of rhythm. As the music reached a crescendo, I couldn't stop the throbbing wave that rose up from my loins until I could hold back no longer. The choir sang 'amen, amen' as I began to come. The Odd Job Man was also climaxing, the two of us entwined in each other's arms like it was some sort of religious moment.

'Hallelujah,' I screamed. 'Hallelujah!'

The Odd Job Man smothered my mouth with his hand till the shuddering died down. I was in a state of deep, deep shock. Then the slow realisation of what I had just done dawned on me as a huge raft of sperm mixed with my own juice, ran down my leg and formed a small pool on the ground. I stood absolutely numb. Unable to move. Yes, maybe that was it. I was in a trance. I had been hypnotised or something. He had used some magical art on me, or maybe slipped something into my tea at afternoon recess. There had to be a reason for the travesty of the event. But that thought wasn't helping much as I stood there, my twat totally ravaged by his gigantic cock. How was I to get out of here and retain my dignity?

I grabbed the now-soggy plans for the sets and lighting, and handed them to him. 'If you could peruse these,' I said, 'and let me know if there are any problems.' I buttoned up my blouse, pulled my skirt down to cover my naked thighs (could not find my knickers), turned and without so much as a backward glance, walked very slowly out into the rain as if nothing had happened.

Once outside, I jumped on my bike and rode like a mad person, lightning flashing all around me. 'Strike me down dead,' I cried out. 'Put me out of my misery.' My legs pedalled like the devil was after me. Swerving through the traffic, I nearly went under a bus. I rode on and on as sperm edged its way down my legs, mingling with the pouring rain.

When I reached my front door I ran inside and straight into the shower. I stood there letting the water stream onto my face. I reached for the soap to scrub away any trace of the tragic event, only when my hand reached into my twat I found myself, as if by some magic or unseen force, reliving the event until suddenly I was coming again. Oh god. This is so gross.

Sitting here in the kitchen. Rain still pouring. Cat from next door sitting licking his arse. He is looking at me now as if he knows. Cats have a sixth sense, I think. At least he's not spraying me. At least it's helping me take my mind off my own pussy. Sort of. Suddenly very tired. Need to go to bed.

2 am. Can't sleep. Tossing and turning. Tried ringing Alison, but there was no answer. I need to talk to her. Ask her if I could be committed to some place in the country. Spend some quality time in an asylum.

Oh god. School tomorrow. I can't take another sick day. What am I going to do now? How am I ever going to face him again? How am I going to handle the situation? How could I have sunk so low? How could I have betrayed the trust of the school like that – like a common slut? And worse still. A thought gnawing at my brain, worming its way through the dark recesses of my mind: it was the best fuck I'd ever had.

Thursday

6 am. Hardly slept a wink. And knocking myself off every half an hour doesn't seem to have helped.

No sign of the Odd Job Man when I arrived on my bike. I could hear him – always in the distance – tapping away on some pipe or other, on the ride-on mower. Clip, clip, clip on the privet hedge.

Found myself drifting off in class, reliving each moment of the scene in the boiler room, that big cock sliding into my wetness. Had to force myself to concentrate.

Every time the staffroom door opened, I panicked. Ann asked me what the problem was, I told her I was overtired due to riding the bike to school. She offered to give me a lift every day. That was very sweet of her. She is such a nice person. Anyway, she asked about the lighting and sets, had I spoken to Jack? For a few moments I couldn't even open my mouth, then I told her that preliminary discussions were under way. She was pleased.

Drama club . . . group read the script by the fat girl and friends. It was hard for me to concentrate. I kept looking towards the door, waiting for the Odd Job Man to come in. What if he had something to fix or came in to discuss the lighting? Where is he? Every now and then I wandered to the door to look out, but he was nowhere to be seen. He is doing this on purpose. He is harassing me by not harassing me. He must know that I am thinking litigation. Surely he can't believe I would let this whole thing go?

Amanda and Sheridan asked me who I was looking for. I couldn't even respond. My mind is a total blank. I am paralysed, completely immobilised by the whole awful situation.

Heard Ann suggest that another song was needed. Amanda yelled out, 'Hey, we know one.' Then she and Sheridan began to sing that short dick man song loudly. I came out of my reverie and shut them up. The bell rang for the end of school. I could not believe it. This is worse than I could have dreamed. THE ODD JOB MAN IS IGNORING ME!!!

2 am. Tossing and turning – no amount of fingering is allowing me to sleep. Still reliving the whole dreadful scenario. And on top of that, he never had the decency to face me. This is outrageous. This is totally unacceptable behaviour. It's got hairs on it. I'm going to have to do something. He is not going to get away with this flagrant use of his power. If he comes near me again, charges will be laid – sexual harassment, indecent exposure, carnal knowledge . . . I'm sure there is lots more!

Friday

Why, why, why? Just when I had him in my clutches. What led to this terrible turn of events? Why does everything I do turn into a big pile of doggy do? Maybe I should have planned my strategy a little better.

Felt the need to confront the Odd Job Man in person, about what he'd done, and inform him of my plans re any further harassment which may lead to a court case. He needed to be warned of his culpability in such a situation and he needed to take responsibility for his actions.

His car was in my parking spot when I arrived. I considered this to be a complete slap in the face and abuse of my person. It just added to my rancour. He was thumbing his nose at me and he was not going to get away with it. Once again it was obvious he was avoiding me. I had not actually laid eyes on him since the unfortunate mishap in the boiler room. I decided to give him fair warning and suggest he find a good lawyer.

In my spare period, I went to look for him. I crossed the oval, my high heels plunging into the lawn slowing my progress, and headed into that dark and dank place known as the garden shed. I could hear some movement inside. I took a deep breath and swung open the door with authority. The Odd Job Man was standing on a chair fixing a light bulb. He said nothing as I screamed out 'If you ever come near me again I'll –' I think that was as far as I got before his large member slid into my mouth . . .

It's the first time I have seen Dana totally lost for words. She had dropped in after work to tell me about her Collette Dinnigan. For fully ten seconds her mouth opened and shut like some flapping turtle on its way to the mating grounds in Zanzibar.

'Are you insane?' she eventually blurted out. 'Are you out of your fucking tree? You shagged the janitor in the boiler room at school and then sucked him off in the garden shed?'

'Well that's just it,' I lied, 'he isn't a janitor, as it turns out. He's actually the son of a wealthy industrialist and he's just filling in for Mr Hedges because . . . their fathers fought in the war together.'

She hit the deck in paroxysms of laughter. 'Is that what he told you?' she said. 'That he's really the heir to a great fortune? Some men will say anything to get into your pants. Anyway,' she went on, 'was it good? What was his dick like? At least you're getting a root. That should take your mind off Jamie for a minute.'

Jamie? Oh my god. Realised I hadn't even thought about him for twenty-four hours. What would Dana tell Jamie?

'I believe I'm in love,' I blurted out. 'And so is he. This is the man of my dreams.'

She stared at me. 'The *rubbish* man?' She began laughing. 'You and the *rubbish* man?' Now she was hysterical. 'So what will you wear for a wedding dress?' she screamed. 'A green garbage bag? And maybe you could roll down the aisle in a wheelie bin.' There was no stopping her now. 'And carry white plastic bags instead of flowers, and we can all throw bits of rubbish at you instead of rice.'

I yelled at her to shut up. I told her that Jack was not a garbageman. 'I would not sink so low.' Once again she reminded me of the dwarf at the club. 'No, this is different,' I said. I repeated the story I told Larry, about the gold mines in the Congo, etc., with a bit of embellishment: 'We're going off to Ireland to live in his castle.' Did I go too far yet again?

She stared at me for a few moments then grinned in that sort of sly, I've got your number girlie, way. 'Well,' she said, 'if that's the case, we'll have to meet him, won't we? I know,' she said, 'I'm having a barbie next Friday week. A few of my new best friends. Lorelei and Jamie will be there, of course. I wasn't going to ask you because you'd do all the bunny-boiler stuff, but now that you're completely over Jamie, it should be good fun. Give you a chance to get to know

Lorelei better. She's so sweet. Bring along what's-his-name.'

'Jack,' I said. 'It's Jack.'

'Maybe he could bring some photos of the castle . . . if it's all true,' she added. 'What do you think?'

'Be lovely,' I blurted out. 'Jack and I would love to.' And she was out the door, hot on her mobile.

Now it was my turn to flap my mouth. What a fucking stupid thing to say! Why did I open my big trap? What am I going to do now? The immediate solution is to kill myself – but nobody would find me for days and the cat would eat my cheeks, which means Jamie couldn't sob over the open coffin.

Need to call Alison. She has to see me. She has to tell me how to get out of this mess.

Tried, but still only the answer machine.

Saturday

There is no way I can ask the Odd Job Man to the barbie at Dana's. Just have to think of another plan – maybe involving a dying aunt or something – which requires my urgent attention in the Outback. Oh god. Why do I keep getting myself into these messes? Speaking of which, where is the Odd Job Man? Why hasn't he contacted me?

It's not as if he doesn't know where I live for Christ's sake. He could have sent flowers, at least. A note with a quick 'thank you'. I mean, you can't just fuck someone willy-nilly and then ignore them as though it never happened. Maybe he doesn't know my phone number. He could find out easily enough. It's in the book. I mean, a small conversation, like 'How are you? Did you enjoy your come the other day? I liked it a lot when you sucked me off, thank you very much. Was it good for you too? Nice weather we're having.' Something. Anything. It's like I'm just a receptacle for his love juice. No. This will not do. This is totally unacceptable behaviour.

I wonder if he works Saturdays. Maybe I should ride down to the school. I don't think my twat could take it, quite frankly. Not after that pounding. Maybe a quick taxi there and back. I mean, he could be feeling really terrible. Fretting. He must have some thoughts on the matter, surely.

No sign of him at school. This is unbelievable. I wonder where he lives. I don't even know his second name. And what am I doing thinking about the Odd Job Man when I haven't even got a plan re ruining Jamie's wedding?

Sunday

Shit. Forgot it was Mum's birthday. Realised as soon as I cycled up the driveway and the nieces and nephews were all in their party clothes. 'Where's Grandma's present?' they screeched in unison. 'What did you buy her?'

I was up the well-known creek. But some quick thinking saved the day. Mum is one of those people who loves unconditionally and always thinks the best of people, so I pretty much got away with it. As I went into the kitchen, I gave her a hug and said, 'Happy birthday. The thing I bought you didn't arrive. It was being delivered, and I waited in all day yesterday, and they promised it would be there, and I kept ringing the delivery van, but it had broken down on the freeway and then the guy who was fixing the wheel was run over by a truck and had to be taken to hospital and some villains ransacked the van and stole all the contents. Can you believe that?'

'Hmm, that's interesting,' said my jerk of a brother-in-law. 'That's the same excuse you gave last year.'

I stared at him with as much contempt as I could muster. 'Are you suggesting that I would forget my own mother's birthday?'

'Yes,' he said with a smug look on his face.

I ignored him. I was not going to spoil Mum's special day because of that fuckwit. I was above that sort of behaviour.

As it turned out, my sister had cooked lunch to give Mum a rest. Not that there was any joy to be had in that. My sister belongs to the same school of cooking as my mother. As she proudly states herself, 'Mum taught me everything I know.' Imagine admitting something like that. The mind boggles.

Started off with a prawn cocktail consisting of limp iceberg lettuce leaves and tinned shrimps whose 'use by' could well have predated the Crimean War, drowned in Thousand Island Dressing. Kids thought it was 'delicious, Mum' and gobbled it down. I worry for their future sometimes.

I stupidly feigned a liver complaint, which gave my brother-in-law the perfect ammunition to harass me about losing my licence and having a drinking problem, so I asked him whether he'd had a chance to see the brain specialist yet about his personality bypass, which had obviously gone wrong. As usual the exchange began to descend into insults which could have turned nasty, but the situation was saved by the pressure cooker blowing its lid off. It smashed into the ceiling, bringing down half the plaster, then ricocheted off the sink and smashed all the cups and saucers. Fortunately I was able to use this incident to my advantage. Told Mum that, guess what? The gift that was held up on delivery was indeed a new pressure cooker. My mother hugged me and asked me what brand it was. Said I couldn't remember. My brother-in-law looked at me as if I was a cockroach. Mum got all teary and said how lovely it was to have the family around etc. That shut my brother-in-law up.

My sister declared triumphantly that, although the cooker had blown, the content (what might once have been a cauliflower in a previous incarnation) was cooked to perfection. It clambered onto the plate as a sort of mushy soup over the now catatonic roast beef. She managed to scrape the potatoes out of the pan without too much effort, and the pumpkin, although a little black, was still quite recognisable because of its orange colour. Dad made a sandwich out of his dinner, declaring the whole meal to be a sensation. Am I related to these people, I sometimes wonder. Is it possible that I was adopted, as I'd always hoped?

Dessert was flummery — made of whipped jelly crystals and evaporated milk, which made the kids go mental. By the time the candles were lit on the cake they were jumping from couch to couch singing 'Born in the USA'.

I mentioned to my sister that perhaps food colouring and additives were not the best thing to give to children whose personalities could be said to be fragile. My brother-in-law interrupted to ask whether I was suggesting his children were out of control, said that I might take a look at my own life if I wanted a discussion about 'control'. Just as it was about to descend into the usual chaos, Dad lit the candles and turned out the light and everyone started to sing 'Happy Birthday' to Mum. Suddenly, there was a vision at the door. An elegant woman, dressed in an immaculate suit, perfectly coiffed hair. We all stared. 'Bon anniversaire, ma chérie,' she said in perfect French.

Completely forgetting about the candles, we all rushed to hug my adorable Aunt Penelope. There was lots of kissing.

Mum was over the moon. She cried. Dad had apparently organised for Aunt Pen to arrive on her birthday as a surprise. What a life she has led – so many stories, so many adventures – as I pointed out to Mum. She's only staying for a week or so, then back off overseas.

Aunt Pen offered to drive me home in her hire car – put the bike in the boot. I was hoping the subject of my adoption would be mentioned now that we were alone but, for whatever reason, it didn't come up. Instead she asked me how I was going at school and whether I enjoyed being a teacher. I lied and said I loved it. I didn't want her to think that I had misused the opportunity she'd given me. She asked after Claire McConnichy, said she would drop in to see her while she was here. Shit. Miss McConnichy will no doubt tell her that I am on notice due to the various incidents during the term. I will have to work harder re the panto, so that my aunt will be proud of me. She is staying at the Windsor Hotel, of course.

Cat from next door has brought a mouse in and is sitting there extremely proudly. Only the mouse isn't dead. He's playing with it, throwing it in the air, as if to get my attention. He's on his back now, holding the poor little thing aloft. Oh gross. Now he's bitten its head off. Talk about attention seeking. I'm going to have a word with the owners.

Great. According to one of the flat-dwellers next door, the people who own the cat left two weeks ago. I knocked on the door of all the units, cat in hand, suggesting that someone might like to take it and/or have it put down or something. Four doors slammed in my face, a dog attacked me, the cat clawed my head as it tried to get away, and I was told to 'Fuck off, cunt' by number 10. So what now? Just given it some sardines which he gobbled up, then a can of tuna which he also demolished. He's now sitting on my lap.

2 am. A totally brilliant plan is forming in my mind re getting Jamie back. Not that some of my other plans have been all that successful... But what if I *did* ask the OJM to the barbecue (he does owe me, after all, what with the flagrant misuse of my body). I could somehow keep the conversation away from the castle in Ireland – maybe warn Dana ahead of time that he gets really angry when people ask about it. Yeah, so far so good. Then I could be all over him like a rash and encourage him to do the same to me... he certainly didn't seem to need too much encouragement in the boiler room. And he is, I suppose, quite cute now that I have a clearer mind about the situation. Yes... maybe I could ask him to do this for me and I won't press charges... I mean, the jury would take my side as the business in the boiler room could be seen as a forced entry situation. Mind you, I could be up shit creek re the debacle in the garden shed. But in any case, if I could get him to go with me to the barbie, Jamie would be beside himself with rage and jealousy. I think this could be my trump card. He will see another man's hands on my body and by the time the sausages are served, Jamie will be mine.

Monday

Got to school early for a change. OJM's car was in my parking space as usual, but I suppose that doesn't count anymore as I can't drive mine. This is going to take some very careful handling. I will of course need to be pleasant at first, then firm re the fact that he owes me. My stomach is churning just at the thought of speaking to him. I am going to have to be in total control so that I don't blurt out something stupid, which could be my undoing. A strategy needs to be put in place. Particularly as my entire future is at stake.

Went to put an ad on the noticeboard re the cat. Thought I might find some soft soul amongst the students who would be willing to take it home. Said some nice things about the cat – cute, good mouser. Didn't mention the facespraying. Girls were standing around the noticeboard laughing as I approached. And then I saw them. My knickers, pinned on the noticeboard with a message: 'Found in the boiler room. Would the owner please explain.' Girls were standing around chuckling. I took the knickers down, saying how disgusting it all was.

'Not yours, are they, Miss?' piped up Amanda. 'Looks about your size.' I ignored her.

How dare he flaunt his own misdemeanours in my face. He will not get away with this.

As if I haven't got enough on my plate, now Miss McConnichy wants me to supervise the Halloween disco for Years 7 and 8 next Friday night. Just because the other staff have got exams to set. She said that with my particular flair for theatrics, she's sure I can come up with an interesting evening. Sue, the phys ed teacher, would help me.

I was about to protest and say that my Friday nights were full when she mentioned how good it would look to the parents that I was doing extracurricular activities that did not involve unseemly behaviour. Blackmail. Told her my aunt was back. She just nodded with that odd look on her face.

Used the Halloween topic to keep 8C amused for a period. Took them off to the library to do some research. The library, which is on the second floor, offers a perfect view of the school grounds. I could surreptitiously look for the Odd Job Man, work out his modus operandi, and present him with my ultimatum: the court appearance or the barbecue – his choice. I waited, I watched, but nothing.

Amanda sidled up to me. 'Who are you looking for, Miss?'

'I'm just admiring the lovely view,' I lied.

'Oh,' said Amanda, 'there's Jack on his mower. Look at the way he straddles the seat. Bet he's a good rider, eh, Miss.'

I told her to sit down. She is such a little slut, unbelievable. I never thought of such things at her age. Well, I thought about them but I certainly never said them out loud. And as I watched him it did cross my mind that I had indeed been straddled by the man on the mower. He was wearing his overalls and a tee shirt. Had this weird sort of feeling, not involving my twat this time, but more a feeling of . . . I don't know . . . perhaps a desire to communicate in some other way than with our genitals.

The girls interrupted me again. Brenda had discovered that on the traditional All Hallows Day, the Druids used to light bonfires and dress up as ghosts and witches to chase away evil spirits. Amanda suggested that, in homage to this medieval tradition, we burn the school down. Sheridan was all for sacrificing one of the Year 7 girls as the centrepiece of the evening. The other girls hooted with laughter, of course, and I reminded A and S that they would not be present anyway as they had been grounded. At this they turned surly and completely bagged the whole idea of Halloween, saying it was for babies.

The rest of the girls are quite excited by it all, particularly as the boys from St Andrew's will be coming. I will organise some appropriate disco music, like 'Monster Mash', 'The Time Warp', 'Thriller', a prize for the best costume, bobbing for apples, passing the pumpkin, maybe a fortune-teller, etc. Good old-fashioned harmless fun. I will indeed show Miss McConnichy that I am a more than worthy member of the staff of St Augustine's. It will also impress my adorable Aunt Pen.

The fat girl and her cronies delivered the panto script. A little boring and predictable, but it's harmless, I suppose. Put a sign on the noticeboard that auditions will be held on Wednesday.

Re cat, asked Ann if she wanted some more pussy in the house. Cheap joke, but she laughed. She said, 'Cats choose, you know. It belongs to you now.'

Great. Just what I didn't want. A pet. Don't even know whether I'm allowed to have one in the house.

Shit. Stayed back after school. Went looking for the Odd Job Man, which I suppose was a little dangerous, although it did make me a tad excited too. Heard a sound coming from the staff loo. Water running as if some cleaning was going on, a lot of seat-banging. Crept in. The door to one of the cubicles was closed but not locked. I pushed it open with gusto, saying, 'You owe me, arsehole.' Only it was Miss White the cookery teacher, with her pants down around her ankles. She just stared at me. I ran out. No point trying to explain. Hope she doesn't report me.

At last. Alison has left a message. She will see me tomorrow night. About bloody time. Cat on the pillow, licked my nose. I think it's a fait accompli. At least it's not spraying anymore. Have to give it a name. Can't think what. Maybe . . . George.

Tuesday

Session with Alison was totally bizarre. She had obviously taken no notice of my recommendation for depilatory treatment – in fact her moustache was growing as voraciously as the infamous Japanese kudzu vine, and her hair was even greyer than I remember, caught up in some sort of bun thing with bits of it hanging out all over the place. She had on her old cardigan and a pleated skirt. I mean, when somebody tells you, with the best of intentions, that you could basically do with a major makeover, you would take at least some of it on board, I would have thought.

She sat there staring at me with those piercing blue eyes and a fixed smile on her face and said nothing. Every now and then her eyelids closed slightly and her voice, when she finally spoke after about ten minutes of silence, was a little thick. I suddenly realised she was up to her eyeballs on some sort of medication. And I'm paying for this shit?

'So, Margaret, what is it you want?'

What a fucking stupid question. I needed to placate Alison at this stage, though, so I smiled back at her. 'I'm here because I obviously need help,' I said.

'In your phone message,' she said thickly, 'you mentioned a court case pending in regard to your drunk driving and you want a letter to the court suggesting you are trying to solve your problems.'

'That's about the size of it,' I said.

She stared at me some more. 'Thing is,' she said, 'I'm not sure that you are trying to deal with your problems. Have you solved the conundrum yet?' she said.

I stared back at her. Would I be here, I wanted to scream out, sitting in this stupid fucking chair, wasting my precious time, if I had solved the fucking conundrum? However, I controlled myself. 'Unfortunately no,' I said. 'I have searched and searched and I'm beginning to wonder if the answer really is in my diary.'

She gave me that fixed smile which was really unnerving. 'I feel quite sure it is,' she said.

'Well,' I said carefully, 'if you really think the answer is there, even though you haven't read my diary, could you please tell me what it is?'

She just sat there with that stupid grin on her face. What happened to the old Alison, the one who seemed to care about my life? This one is just on automatic pilot. I am beginning to wonder if there wasn't some serious brain damage when she catapulted back over the chair.

'You have to find the answers for yourself, Margaret,' she said at last. 'I can only guide you, but I've said all this before. It doesn't seem to be sinking in. However . . .'

Silence reigned once more.

'So bring me up to date,' she finally said, causing me to jump a little. 'Tell me what you've been doing since I saw you last.'

And here I had to be careful. I told her a few snippets, but did not elaborate too much. Didn't tell her about the boiler room/shed fiasco as I'm sure she would have put some weird slant on it. Mentioned the panto and how well that was going, mentioned my great relationship with my parents, talked about school.

She suddenly interrupted: 'Margaret, if we are to continue these sessions, I do not want to hear bullshit. I want you to tell me what is really going on or there is no point.'

Alison swearing like that came as a shock.

'For instance,' she said, 'where were you going when the police picked you up, and why had you been drinking?'

And before I knew it, it was out of my mouth. There is something about Alison that forces the truth out of you. It's those piercing blue eyes. I blurted out the whole sorry tale, about my plan to stop the wedding by telling them I was pregnant etc.

'So nothing's changed then. You have not moved forward in any way,' she said, jotting down notes. 'You are obviously still obsessed with Jamie, even though he is about to marry someone else. Well, I'm willing to see you for another four sessions. If, in that time, I don't feel you have shown any willingness to look deeply into yourself and re-evaluate, I will terminate these sessions. You are, of course, entitled to find another psychologist, if you so desire. It's all entirely up to you. And that's our time for this evening,' she said like a recorded message. Then she picked up her bag and left the room.

What the fuck is going on?

Wednesday

Panto auditions. Amanda and Sheridan thought the script was putrid. Why would anyone give up all that power and money for love, particularly when she is a total bitch? You can't change overnight according to Sheridan. Amanda backed her up, saying the whole thing was a crock and arguing that the only happy ending would be for the princess to realise what a cunt she is and hang herself from the top turret. Suggested that Amanda's mother wash her mouth out with soap and water. She argued and said her mother says 'cunt' all the time. Sent her outside for five minutes.

In my heart I had to agree with A and S, but the

numbers were against me. I told them that if they were morally opposed to the panto, perhaps they could work behind the scenes and not take part. They stopped complaining then. Everyone wanted to play the princess, of course, but Sheridan insisted that she should play it and in fact I had to admit she read better than anyone else. She also insisted that Amanda play the swineherd/prince. Nobody wanted to challenge that. I think they are all a little afraid of A and S. Brenda the overweight will play the queen, Trudy the moron will play the king, and Wendy the malnourished from birth is the jester. The minor parts were sorted out with the rest of the troupe and everyone has to double as the crowd and the visiting princes. Sheridan asked about the lighting and sound. I told them it was all under control.

Shit. Am I going off my brain? Maybe I need new glasses. Misplaced my diary again. I was frantic. Eventually found it under a pile of books on the table in the hall where we had been rehearsing. I must be more careful. I would hate anyone to read it.

I have to make a move on the OJM pretty damn soon. If only I could find him. Decided to leave a note on his car with my phone number and a message: 'Lighting and sound would be appreciated ASAP. Perhaps we could meet after school in the hall, discuss the finer details.' He will probably need my help. I could maybe hold the tools for him and/or the ladder, and if there was a blackout or something, he could once again slip his giant cock – oh my god. Can't believe this crap is coming from my mind. And now I'm wet again. Ride home will cure all that.

Mum rang. Aunt Pen is taking us all to yum cha on Sunday. Had to explain to Mum what yum cha is. She was very relieved when I told her. God only knows what she thought it was. I am looking forward to Sunday. It's wonderful to have someone amazing and talented in the family. Someone to look up to. Maybe Sunday is the day she'll announce to all that she is my real mother.

11 pm. The Odd Job Man still hasn't called. Unbelievable. What game is he playing?

Thursday

Amazing. Walked into the hall for rehearsal today and there it was. The lights all hanging from the lighting grid according to my plan. The sound system had been set up and the canvas backdrop had been dragged out of the storeroom. I asked Ann if she'd done it.

'No,' she said, 'It was Jack.'

What does this mean? Obviously he must realise I am litigation bound and he is trying to suck up to me. Hmm . . . haven't had a good licking for a while.

Oh god. There is definitely something evil happening in my brain. Maybe it's a tumour.

Read through the whole panto. Have to admit that Brenda has done an all right job. A very nice scene when the swineherd and the princess meet for the first time. They are in the garden. The swineherd, dressed as a prince, has his back to her and a long cloak on, so she can't see him.

PRINCESS: (*singing*) Someday my Prince will come.

(*Sees the Swineherd in the garden.*) What are you doing in my garden? This is private. Can't you read the signs?

SWINEHERD: I'm sorry, but I'm blind.

(*Princess goes up to the sign.*)

PRINCESS: Here – this is what it says: P-R-I-V-A-T-E. Now you know. So go and wait somewhere else or I'll have you –

(*Swineherd turns around and takes off his cloak to reveal handsome young man. He smiles at her.*)

SWINEHERD: You'll have me what?

(*The Princess stares at the handsome young man.*)

PRINCESS: (*to audience*) He is very handsome, don't you think? But I can't let him see that I'm attracted to him. (*to Prince*) I'll have you boiled in oil.

SWINEHERD: Oh goodie. The hotter the better. I like it like that.

PRINCESS: In that case I'll have you flogged.

SWINEHERD: Fine by me. I have very thick skin. In fact, I always find that if flogging is done correctly, it tickles.

(*The Princess is thrown off guard.*)

PRINCESS: In that case I'll just throw you in the dungeon till you rot.

SWINEHERD: Thank you. I will enjoy the isolation. There is nothing better than being on your own. It's good for the soul. Do you mind if I take a good book?

PRINCESS: Just a minute. You said you were blind.

SWINEHERD: Alas, I'm afraid you've caught me out. You must be very clever. And you're right, I'm not blind. I see everything. And I always recognise a beautiful young woman when I see her.

PRINCESS: (*fluttering her eyelashes*) And have you seen one lately?

SWINEHERD: Well, that depends. Beauty is only skin deep, after all. There are many pretty girls around, but true beauty comes from within. Alas, the only girls I've come across in my travels are shallow, vain, selfish and mean.

PRINCESS: Oh really? I don't know anyone like that.

SWINEHERD: What about the Princess who lives in this castle? I've heard she's the meanest woman in the world.

PRINCESS: Oh no. She's sweet and warm and wonderful and nice.

SWINEHERD: Then maybe it won't be such a bore meeting her. I'm a Prince, you see, from a foreign land. My father insisted that I meet this Princess. But I've heard so many bad stories about her.

PRINCESS: Maybe you'll be surprised. You'll just have to wait and see.

(*Song: 'Something's Coming' from* Westside Story.)

Stayed back after school. Now at least I had an excuse. I could thank the OJM for the sound/lighting, mention the possibility of charges being laid, then invite him to the barbecue at Dana's.

Looked everywhere. Even went down to the garden shed. Relived every moment of the fellatio that was forced upon me in this quiet place. My fingers started sliding into my knickers. Stopped myself just in time. Knew that I would have a squishy ride home. It's now nearly a week since his member was in my mouth. Still no sign of him.

A solicitor's letter was waiting for me at home, a letter demanding $2000 for damage to Lorelei's car. Right, that's it. I have had Lorelei up to pussy's bow. I am going to put that slut in her place.

Dropped into the local fish shop before I went to the perfumery. The dumb slut from the Rhine was behind the counter when I sauntered in. There were several customers in the shop, and she was serving one of them, a rather large woman in a fur coat. I asked the woman how many animals had to be skinned to cover her excess adipose tissue. The woman was not sure exactly what I meant, and nor was Lorelei, but she apologised on my behalf anyway. Said I was mental. The fat beaver left in a huff.

'Can I help you with anything?' Lorelei said through tight lips.

'Actually there is,' I said loudly. I pulled the solicitor's letter out of my bag. 'It's this load of crap here.' I threw the letter at her and told her very politely that she had no proof that it was me, so it was all bullshit.

She protested and said that she knew it was me. She knows I wear Purple Passion lipstick, Jamie told her. So does half the country, I pointed out.

By now the other customers in the shop had started to sniff the air in confusion. The delicate aromas of Joy, Fidgi and Miss Dior were being overpowered by the bag of fish guts and prawn heads that I had retrieved from the bins out the back of the fishmonger's and placed surreptitiously under the counter near a heating outlet. One woman started to gag and ran outside. Lorelei could also smell the offensive material, I could tell, but she was not sure of its source.

'Did you actually see me?' I asked.

Lorelei said nothing.

'That being the case,' I said in a very modulated voice, 'why don't you take this letter and cram it directly up your fundament.'

On the way out I pretended to trip over a display of Yves St Laurent's Paris, which sent the bottles flying like missiles. I said I'd be suing them for putting their display in such a ridiculous spot – it was a danger to man and beast. Lorelei was hiding under the counter when I left. Yes!

Friday

Spent the day setting up for the Halloween disco in the hall. Miss White the cookery teacher organised the supper table and the jugs of punch. The students from 10A, supervised by the art department tart, hung the decorations – broomsticks, skeletons etc. Pumpkins were provided by the local supermarket to add atmosphere and the local pub supplied the barrel for the apple bobbing. With the sound set up and the CDs loaded, everything was ready to go.

Suddenly occurred to me that the OJM would be here this evening. He would have to sweep up the rubbish, close up the hall. Tonight I will corner him. What should I wear?

Saturday

Oh the horror . . . Oh awful Halloween, oh night of the long knives. Still under the bed as I write. Hands trembling. Start from the beginning. Set the scene. See if I can make sense of the horrifying events that unfolded on this Day of the Dead.

Got a taxi and arrived at school at six thirty to make sure everything was in place. Decided to go as one of the glamorous witches in *Charmed*, rather than the warts-on-the-nose, broomstick variety. Did the plunging neckline, the follow-me-home-and-fuck-me shoes – thought that when I asked the OJM to the barbecue I would need to have the upper hand.

The hall looked amazing. The tables were now covered

with large jugs of fruit punch, savouries, sandwiches, the usual. Sue the phys ed teacher was there early as well. She was still in her tracksuit, whistle around her neck. Hadn't bothered to enter into the festive spirit. I often wonder about phys ed teachers. They seem to have no idea there is a world outside of throwing the javelin and putting the shot.

Kids started arriving just before seven. They had all gone to a lot of trouble with their costumes. The boys from St Andrew's mostly went for the Harry Potter look, with a few ghosts, werewolves and zombies thrown in. Among the girls there were witches, Hermiones, black cats and ghosts, plus two girls dressed in green leotards wearing pumpkins on their heads, which I thought was very creative. Everyone was a little awkward at the start, boys over one side of the room, girls over the other. A game of pass the zucchini got the ball rolling and everyone mixing, then some apple-bobbing and the whole evening was under way. Put the disco music on and they started dancing, all the girls together first, then the boys joined in. I was very pleased with how things were going.

About 8 pm we awarded prizes for the best costumes. One of the Year 7 girls who came as a skeleton won (although it turned out she was just anorexic with a black dress on). Would have given first prize to the pumpkin girls, but they were nowhere to be seen. I figured with the weight of those Queensland blues on their heads, they had probably left early.

About eight thirty Sue said she was going out for a smoke. Unbelievable. I mean, these sports people give all these lectures about health and fitness and yet they keep fagging on. Anyway, that was fine by me. I'd have a chance to take a break later when she came back. That would be my opportunity to go looking for the Odd Job Man rather than hanging around afterwards and having to talk to him while he swept the floors.

When Sue returned I went outside in my quest for the OJM. Had my speech all ready. I would be firm but fair, point out that I felt I had been taken advantage of in a sexual manner blah blah blah, and although I wasn't a bitter person, I felt he owed me and I needed a favour. I had practised all afternoon so that I wouldn't make any mistakes.

Outside in the cool air, I looked around. The moon was full and cast an eerie glow over the school grounds. Shadows flickered and changed like phantoms flitting through the night. A slight wind was moving in the tall plane trees . . . There was a chill in the air. I shuddered involuntarily. It was indeed All Hallows Day, the Day of the Dead. I could feel something in the air. Sorcery. Witchcraft. I should have trusted my instincts. Something told me to go back into the hall, into the light and the warmth where there were people and safety, but another side of me was crying out that this was a night for adventure, for risk-taking. And I was in fact feeling very horny. Started thinking about that giant cock and how it felt in my mouth. Why, why, why did I let my genitals get in the way of common sense?

There was no sign of the Odd Job Man near the hall. I looked high and low for him. Then I heard something in the distance. Sounded like tapping on a pipe. I began to follow the sound. The tapping became louder. It was coming from the boiler room. A warning was going off in my brain, a voice crying out to me, 'Turn back, turn back now!' But I was drawn to that dark, dank, place where the Odd Job Man's fingers had first found their quarry. I couldn't stop myself. I ventured in, as if drawn by the devil himself. I realised I wanted him again. I wanted to feel him thrusting into me. I was not in control anymore. Down, down I went, tip toeing quietly on the steps. I would surprise him. I could almost feel his hot breath, his tongue searching my mouth, his hands on my body, his hardness pressed against me. I was hot. I was dripping. I was ready.

The sound of tapping got louder. Metal on pipe. He was there. He knew I was coming. He was waiting for me. Oh joy. In a moment I would be taken, ravaged once more. I would cry out in protest, but he would have his way. Oh glorious night.

Then I heard it. That awful sound, warning me of what was to come. I heard a woman's voice moaning, crying out in pleasure. I should have stopped, I should have turned back, but curiosity got the better of me. I was driven forward until a terrible sight confronted me. Oh evil Halloween! Oh Day of the Dead. Oh another drink . . .

In the gloom I could see the shape of a rather corpulent woman seated on a small workbench in the boiler room, her skirt up, her legs ajar – one foot on the boiler pipe, the other on the back of a chair, the buckle of her undone belt hitting the water pipe as she vibrated uncontrollably. Another figure moved in the darkness. Just then the moon came from behind a cloud and illuminated the gruesome scene below. Now I could see clearly the perfectly coiffed head of my Aunt Penelope, her immaculately manicured nails holding open two chunky thighs, and her tongue jammed right up Miss McConnichy's crack.

'Keep going, Pen,' cried Miss McConnichy. 'To the left, yes, that's it . . . I'm coming. Oh yes . . . oh yes . . . oh yeeees . . .'

Aghhhh! Oh anus horribilus. Oh awful cunnilingus. How I managed to make my legs move, I don't know. I backed out of that evil place as silently as I had entered. I was in shock.

My Aunt Penelope, the woman I admired more than anyone in the world, was muff-diving my principal.

I stood in the quadrangle trying to catch my breath, trying to make sense of what I had just seen. How long I stood there I don't know. But suddenly, all hell broke loose. I heard frantic whistle-blowing from the hall. Something was amiss. I ran and, as I did, I stumbled over a pile of bottles that had been left on the lawn. Stollies. Alarm bells went off in my head.

What greeted me in the hall was something akin to a bacchanalian orgy. Students writhed on the floor with each other, tongues down each other's throats, fingers in forbidden places, one girl vomiting in a corner. They were drunk. Drunk as skunks. 'The fruit punch,' cried Sue, 'someone has tampered with the fruit punch!'

The phys ed teacher and I tried with all our might to pull the writhing bodies apart in order to administer coffee, water, aspirin, but it was all too late. The parents had arrived to pick up their beloved offspring. Oh, what a scandal.

And to top it off, Miss McConnichy, looking as if butter wouldn't melt in her mouth, arrived and blamed me for the debacle. Miss High and Mighty Pussy Bumper behaving as if she was above condemnation. And *she* wishes to see *me* in her office on Monday for an explanation. She then talked to the parents, trying to placate everyone, claiming that the students were not drunk but simply enthusiastic and full of the joys of spring. How she got away with it I'll never know, but the parents seemed to accept her explanation.

The OJM came and helped clean up the hall. I didn't feel like speaking to him. Didn't feel like speaking to anyone. I was numb. Sue offered to drive me home, but I said I'd be fine. I wandered off into the dark night, wishing I could hide away, wishing I was under my bed in the fluff, in my shoe-box world.

I sat on the seat at the bus stop just staring at the moon, that heinous orb which had cast such awful light on those monstrous events in the boiler room. Better that I had been blinded, my eyes poked out by demons, than to witness such horrors. My thoughts turned to the fiasco in the hall. Who would want to spoil a night of good clean wholesome fun? And as the moon went behind a cloud, it dawned on me. Of course. The two Queensland blues who had disappeared early in the evening. Sheridan and Amanda.

A car pulled up. It was the Odd Job Man. He opened the door. I got in without a word. He drove me home. He came inside, made me a cup of tea. I sat there staring straight ahead, unable to expunge that terrible sight in the boiler room. I thought about Mum. Did she know? How had she managed to hide this from the family all these years? And worse still, how was I going to face Aunt Pen at yum cha tomorrow?

The Odd Job Man suddenly interrupted my reverie: 'Come on now, it can't be all that bad.' I burst into tears at that point. He gave me some tissues. And then he said something really strange: 'Why don't you go and lie under your bed for a while. You'll feel much better.'

I stared at him.

'Good place to be when things go wrong. It's what I used to do when I was a kid,' he said. 'Pull the fluff around me. Used to call it my shoe-box world. Used to make those scenes –'

'With the cellophane,' I said.

He nodded. There was silence for a long time.

'Would you like to come to a barbecue with me next Friday?' I mumbled.

'I'd like that,' he said and left.

Sunday

Rang Mum, tried to get out of yum cha. She insisted. Aunt Pen would be so disappointed. It would be her last chance to be with the family before she flew back to Paris. And the table had been booked.

Thought if I arrived late I could just go to my seat without any fuss as everyone would have started, but Aunt Pen got up from her chair and gave me a big kiss on the mouth. I'm sure I could taste Miss McConnichy's vagina juice. I tried not to gag.

I couldn't eat. I just stared at that elegant tongue as it licked the sauce from a dim sim, knowing that only hours earlier it had been lapping at the labia of the woman in charge of my employment. Mum asked me what was wrong. She noticed I was very quiet. I wanted to stand up and scream out, 'There's a Lesbian at our table!', but I refrained. Said it was something I'd eaten. Bad choice of words – I gagged involuntarily.

Aunt Pen mentioned that she'd run into Claire McConnichy, who had said how well I was doing at St Augustine's and how brilliantly the panto was coming along. I wanted to scream out something about her relationship with the aforementioned. But I didn't. I held on to my terrible secret.

Even my brother-in-law commented on my subdued behaviour, and then asked me whether I'd remembered the pressure cooker. I mumbled something about it being on its way. He said, 'So is Christmas.' But I couldn't raise a retort. I think he was quite disappointed. I managed to swallow a couple of pork buns, then made my excuses to leave. Said I wasn't feeling well.

A bunch of freesias on the doorstep when I got home. My favourite flowers. The perfume lifts my heart with joy.

He remembered. Oh, my wonderful Jamie. He must have known in his heart that I was down. Rang Jamie and thanked him. Said it wasn't him and hung up. Wonder who it could have been?

Monday

Laid awake all night thinking about the gross sight in the boiler room. Decided it was my duty to 'out' my Aunt Penelope. Decided that the family should know about her deviant behaviour. And more to the point, I needed to find out if I was adopted, as I had always hoped, and whether I carried the mutant gene.

Meeting with Miss McConnichy. Couldn't look her in the face. Of course the blame was laid squarely at my feet re the Halloween fiasco. Why had I left the hall? Where was I? Why had I shirked my responsibility? It was on the tip of my tongue to scream out, 'And where were you, madam? In the boiler room with my auntie's head up your snatch!' But I managed to hold back. I needed to handle this with some dignity.

She asked me if I had any suspects re the vodka. I laid the blame squarely on Amanda and Sheridan. Said I believed they were the guilty parties. They were summoned to the office.

Of course they denied it. Said they were at Sheridan's place all night. A sleepover. I asked whether there was anyone who could vouch for that. At this point Miss McConnichy stepped in. She obviously had the new library in mind. Suggested that we take their word for it, not pursue the matter any further.

Unbelievable. Amanda and Sheridan smirked as they left. And now my job is on the line. Miss McConnichy suggested that if things did not improve by the end of the year she would have no choice but to terminate my employment, regardless of her affection for my aunt. I was about to challenge her re the nature of her 'affection' when Miss White the cookery teacher came in with the morning tea. The conversation was closed. Those little sluts. Right. That's it. They will feel the full force of my wrath. I have put a notice on the board. A special meeting of the drama club is called for tomorrow.

OJM came up to me after school. Asked me if I was feeling better. I said yes. He said he hoped I liked the freesias. They're his favourite flowers. The perfume always cheers him up. He hoped it had done the same for me. He smiled, then walked away. I was a bit taken aback.

Went around to Mum and Dad's after school. Decided my Aunt Pen needed to be 'outed' immediately. No more skulking around pretending to be something she was not. Mum needed to be told the truth.

She was reading a Mills and Boon when I came in, fag hanging out of her mouth as usual. Something was on the stove cooking for Dad's tea – either that or she was boiling some old socks. Hard to tell. I started off by asking whether or not I was adopted. Mum insisted that I wasn't. I breathed a sigh of relief. That left me clear to present Mum with the facts about her beloved sister. In the nicest possible way, of course. I hoped she was going to handle it okay.

'Mum,' I said, 'Aunt Pen is a big dyke.'

Mum never even looked up from her book. 'Well of course she is, darling. She's been gay ever since I can remember. We noticed around the time she was five. It's no secret,' she said.

I was dumbstruck. Totally lost for words. 'How come I was never told?' I cried. 'How come I was never let into this awful family secret?'

Mum stopped reading her Mills and Boon and looked at me. 'Well,' she said, 'truth is, Maggie, you're intolerant. You never accept people for what they are. I thought I'd brought you up better, but obviously I made a mistake somewhere along the line. I hope you grow out of it one day.'

And then whatever it was boiled over on the stove. She went into the kitchen. 'Has that pressure cooker arrived yet? Could do with it, darling.'

I was staggered. What a terrible thing for a mother to say to her daughter. Out loud, just like that, suggesting that I was intolerant. Unbelievable.

I rode home on my bicycle. Can life get any worse? And now what? Someone's at the door . . .

Two policemen turned up with a summons. I have to appear in the magistrates court on Friday. Lorelei has taken out an AVO against me for stalking her. Unbelievable!

Tuesday

Special meeting of the drama club at lunchtime. I told the girls I had decided to recast the panto. The part of the princess would now go to the grossly overweight Brenda and the role of the swineherd would now go to the malnourished-from-birth Wendy.

Amanda and Sheridan were stunned. 'But, Miss,' Sheridan cried. 'We never put the vodka in the punch.'

'This has got nothing to do with that,' I lied. 'I just don't think you're right for the roles.' And walked out. I hope they will learn a lesson from this. I am not going to be made a mockery of.

Another weird meeting with Alison. I am seriously concerned about her mental state. Something is definitely wrong with her. She had that stupid smile on her face again.

She sat there, those blue eyes just boring into my brain. Decided not to tell her about the AVO. Felt she might have put the wrong slant on how my life was proceeding, particularly in her highly medicated state.

Told her instead about Aunt Penelope. Not the icky bits in the boiler room, but that I had discovered my favourite aunt was of a gay persuasion. Then I told her about Mum calling me intolerant.

'And how did you feel about that?' said Alison, leaning forward on one elbow, which then promptly slipped off the table. She apologised, said it was a coordination problem.

What is going on with her? And there is something else – tiny scabs have appeared on her upper lip. I think Alison is having electrolysis. I mean, what am I going to do in these sessions without those hairs to amuse me?

I told her I thought Mum's suggestion was outrageous. I believed I was very tolerant of other people and went out of my way to accept people for what they were. I was a teacher, after all. A very giving person.

'I see,' said Alison, jotting down notes on her pad. 'All right,' she said next, folding her hands on the desk in a very mannered way, as if she was in some sort of investigative movie, 'if, as you say, you've been studying your diary, what have you gleaned thus far?'

I knew this was a trick question, one which could well see her cancel my sessions, so I chose my words carefully. 'After studying the diary,' I said, 'the only thing I can come up with is that I am basically superior to other people and that creates jealousy and destructive tendencies in them towards me.'

She stared at me for a moment or two, then she noted all that down. 'I see,' she said. 'Yes, of course, that's what you would think.' Which made no sense at all.

Then the weirdest thing happened. She started singing quietly to herself, 'Onward Christian soldiers . . .' Luckily the timer went off. I made a quick escape.

Alison called out as I left, 'Only three more sessions, Margaret. Time is running out.'

I had no idea Alison was into Jesus.

Call from Larry. He was really upset. Apparently his boyfriend has met someone else and is not coming out from San Fran after all. He sounded devastated. I invited him over Thursday night. Kill two birds with one stone. Offer Larry some comfort, thereby proving that I am a caring, sharing person, and find out info re the wedding so that I can formulate my plans.

Message from Mum reminding me that Aunt Pen is leaving tomorrow night. They would pick me up to go the airport. Mum said she would be really upset if I didn't go. Don't know how I'm going to get out of it.

Wednesday

Unbelievable. Dana called in after work. She saw George, who was having his dinner. 'You're not keeping that ugly cat, are you?' she said.

'He's not ugly,' I said, 'he's just . . . different.'

George must have heard. Put his tail in the air and left.

Dana then dropped the bombshell. 'The barbecue is off,' she said. 'Well, not really off, but Lorelei said she wouldn't accept the invitation if you were going to be there, considering the court case pending and because she thinks you are a serious nutter and quite dangerous.'

'But you can't go back on your invitation,' I said.

'Well, I just have,' she said. 'That's the way it is.'

'But I've asked the um . . . Jack,' I said.

'I'm sorry,' she said 'You shouldn't have behaved so badly!'

'I behaved badly?' I screamed. 'What about that shop girl slut, stealing my man? Where is the justice in that?'

'See?' she said. 'You are totally out of control. I can't have you upsetting my guests. And if I were you I'd get another shrink. The one you've got is obviously not helping.' And she swept out the door.

What a fucking cheek. Now what? All the trouble I have been to. All the pain and angst I've had re asking the Odd Job Man to her barbecue. Having to witness that terrible scene in the boiler room, having my job on the line for leaving the hall. And all for nothing. What am I going to do now?

Just back from the airport. Tried to act as though Aunt Pen was a normal everyday person. She gave me a big hug and said that I must come to Paris. That she would show me the sights. On the tip of my tongue to mention the sight I'd already seen, but held back. I muttered something about my having an important career to tend to. She laughed and said something really weird. 'Oh, Maggs,' she said, 'you're not cut out to be a teacher. You don't want to end up like poor old Claire.' I mean, this is the woman whose flaps she was licking the other night. I have a feeling that my aunt is not only a lesbian but just uses people for sex. And what does she mean, I'm not cut out to be a teacher?

Thursday

Saw the OJM as I cycled up to school. Told him the barbecue was off. Didn't tell him the reason. He asked me if I'd still like to go out somewhere. Maybe dinner or the movies. Thought it was a bit of a cheek and extremely presumptuous of him. I mean, one would have to be at the end of one's rope before going out with a man who empties garbage for a living. But then thoughts of sitting in the back row of the theatre flashed immediately to mind, the Odd Job Man's large digits delving into my wetness, my hand unzipping his fly and releasing the monster that lies within . . . Am I being led by my genitalia at this point? Never mind. Perhaps my brain needs a rest. For some reason I said yes.

Amanda and Sheridan never turned up for drama. The other girls appeared a little nervous. Brenda declared that she'd thought about it and really didn't want to be the princess, and Wendy said she didn't want to be the swineherd. I suspect some serious bullying has gone on here from A and S. I told the girls not to be intimidated. They were not convinced, but said they'd rehearse the new parts anyway. Told Ann re the change of cast when she came in for the music. She said that Amanda and Sheridan had sworn they didn't tamper with the punch. I told Ann that frankly I didn't believe them. Brenda and Wendy were truly terrible as the swineherd and princess. But those brats need to be taught a lesson.

And another sterling opportunity arose. Went to the bottle shop after work and ran into the hairdresser and the butcher's wife. They were stocking up on their usual — trolleys full of vodka, gin and mixers. No wonder Amanda and Sheridan are the way they are. I mean, really.

The slags asked how their little darlings were progressing. I waxed lyrical about how much they'd improved in the last few months and I was sooo pleased that they were able to come to the Halloween disco last week. I saw them look at each other. 'Really?' said the butcher's wife. 'We thought they were studying at a friend's place all evening.'

Bullseye. That'll teach those two.

Larry came over for dinner. He is so sweet. Asked me how my relationship was going. I lied and said everything was wonderful, rolling my eyes in a meaningful way. He looked at my hand to check for the engagement ring. I said it was still being made. He seemed to buy that.

I asked him re the devastation he felt at his relationship breaking up, and he started to cry. I offered him a few words of comfort, like: it obviously wasn't meant to be; time heals everything; plenty more fish, blah blah. Then I managed to draw him around to the subject of the wedding. I needed to know if there was any information relevant to the ongoing dilemma of how to stop the proceedings and win Jamie back now that my barbecue plans had come unstuck.

Larry eventually pulled himself together. He said everything was going smoothly. He mentioned there might be a problem with the time of the wedding, because of a special event at the church. It was a saint's day or something. Then he came up with some information that was truly sensational. It was just what I wanted to hear. He said he'd been trying to organise the girl coming out of the cake thing, but couldn't find anyone suitable. There were plenty of strippers around, but he wanted something tasteful. He had a particular idea in mind. 'Pity,' he said. 'It could have been such fun.'

I saw the opportunity, I took it. I suggested to Larry that, if he could organise the cake, I could organise the girl. Said I had a friend, an actress with a great body, who I'm sure would be interested in the gig. He was delighted. He said he had a designer mate, Christopher, who would make the cake.

Couldn't concentrate on the rest of the evening. Had visions of myself naked, my body covered with cream, rising triumphantly out of the cake. Jamie rushing forward, licking me from head to toe. Oh, what an amazing moment it would be.

Friday

Magistrates court. Unbelievable. Lorelei and Jamie there. The things she said about me were totally outrageous. There was no proof that I had written stuff on her car, I pointed out, and the magistrate accepted that a lot of people wear Purple Passion lipstick, but she did not seem entirely convinced of my innocence. I did have a motive, after all.

I took the opportunity to state my case, explaining that I was totally over Jamie, and the fact that Lorelei had stolen him from me in a most obvious and cruel way was something I had come to terms with, although using her father's death, I said, was the lowest way in which to win someone's love. I had started to point out how unsuited they were and what were they going to talk about after sex, when the magistrate shut me up, which amazed me. I was just trying to state the facts. The magistrate said I'd been watching too much television, then told me to sit down.

What did go against me, however, was the phone calls to Lorelei's house, the punch-up and black eye witnessed by her mother, and my recent visit to the perfumery. A bill for $600 worth of Yves St Laurent's Paris was then handed to me. My cry that I'd slipped on something in the shop and would, in fact, be counter-suing fell on deaf ears.

The magistrate decided there was a case to be answered and went with the AVO, putting a two-kilometre radius on any contact.

I was totally outraged. I pointed out that the perfumery is in the mall where I regularly shop.

'Well, you'll just have to shop somewhere else,' said the magistrate.

'But it's four k's to the nearest supermarket,' I said, 'and I've lost my licence.'

'That is your problem,' said the magistrate. 'You should have thought of that when you behaved in the manner you did.' And she was about to bring down the hammer.

I was on my feet in an instant. 'But what if . . . what if I'm somewhere, say in a coffee shop or a restaurant, and the slut –' I corrected myself, 'the plaintiff comes in. What happens then?'

'You would have to leave,' she said.

'Even though I was there first?' I asked.

'Yes,' she said tightly, 'even though you were there first.' The magistrate seemed to be getting a little tense at this point.

'But what if I'm only halfway through my meal? I mean, think of the starving children in China. You can't just waste good food –'

'All right,' the magistrate said slowly, as if trying to control herself, 'if that were the case, you would be entitled to finish your meal before leaving. Now, is there anything else bothering you?' Her lips were getting thinner by the minute.

I did have some other questions, but I thought it was

probably time to call it a day. I shook my head. The magistrate's hammer came down heavily, which I thought was rather rude. It's my life we're dealing with here.

Lorelei was all smiles as she left the court with Jamie. She looked at me with that 'cat that licked the cream' look. I was very tempted to punch her in the mouth. 'Come on, Jamie,' she said. 'We have to get ready for the barbie tonight.' Poor Jamie, being saddled with that tramp. I must save him while there is still time.

So what am I going to talk about with the Odd Job Man tonight? I mean, what could we possibly have in common? Maybe I can involve him in a conversation about the varying strength of garbage bags, different types of disinfectants, floor polish that doesn't build up wax, stuff like that. Thank god we're going to the movies. And at least I might get a shag afterwards.

So what am I going to wear?

Midnight. Hmm. What can I say? I organised to meet the OJM inside the picture theatre. I didn't want to be seen with him, just in case there was anyone there from school. He actually looked quite spunky, I have to say, in that 'rough trade' sort of way — the tight jeans, the leather jacket, chest-hugging tee shirt. I was sorry that I wasn't able to take him to the barbecue. I think Jamie would have been beside himself with jealousy.

I wore a very short skirt and, with all that cycling, my legs are now in great shape. Tight jumper with short sleeves and just a bit of midriff showing. Tummy also in good shape thanks to bike. Weather was pleasant, mild. Spring is definitely here.

Seeing the movie was a good idea. I suggested the back row, pretending to have a problem with my close-up vision, in the hope that his hands would stray between my legs, which were splayed expectantly for most of the movie. I was hoping that the inevitable fingering would take place with me having to stifle the amazing orgasm I would have, so as not to disturb the theatre patrons. But it was not to be. Every now and then our hands touched accidentally or, when he leaned over to whisper something relevant about the movie, his lips sometimes brushed my cheek. Not sure why, but it made me hornier than ever. And that bulge between his legs was weighing heavily on my mind.

After the movie we went back to my house. Not sure what we talked about. I didn't listen to a lot of what he said, stuff about Ireland, growing up poor, the struggles, the fight for Teddy's head, which I thought at first was a toy bear, but realised he was talking about Northern Ireland. His lilting accent was quite captivating, though.

I managed to tell him a lot about myself and we passed the evening very pleasantly – I didn't have to mention the cleaning once. Nothing was mentioned about the boiler room/shed business either. Not a word. It was like it never happened.

And then he said goodnight and left. I was stunned. And so horny. May have to knock myself off to get to sleep. Wonder why he didn't want to shag me? I have no idea.

Saturday

Dana dropped in to tell me all about the barbecue and how sensational it was and how everyone had a fab time, and the highlight of the evening was when Lorelei mimicked me at the court case. Asking the magistrate all those stupid questions. Everyone thought she was sooo funny. Normally I would have been furious, but for some reason this morning I had a nice warm feeling and couldn't be bothered.

Dana went on and on about Lorelei and what a sensation she is and how they're all going out again tonight to the new fish café, which is sooooo expensive and elegant. 'Lorelei is taking all the wedding party. All twenty of us.'

I made no comment. Told Dana I'd been out with Jack and had an amazing night. Told her we'd shagged ourselves stupid.

'Oh, the garbageman with the castle? The heir to the gold mines and coal mines? I told everyone about that. We all had a good laugh.'

I was pissed off, but I covered. Said that I didn't care whether she believed it or not. I was the happiest girl in the world.

'Well,' she said, 'while you're in such a good mood, I need to borrow some casserole dishes and some big plates. I'm throwing a kitchen tea for Lorelei.'

'Oh, I don't think so,' I said. 'I have a restraining order out against me.'

'That's not for your stuff, though,' Dana whined. 'That's for Lorelei in person.'

'Well, quite frankly I don't want that slut anywhere near my crockery, so as far as I'm concerned you can shove Lorelei's kitchen tea up your arse,' I said ever so politely.

Dana stared at me in horror. 'What is your problem?' she said. And stormed out.

Then I had a thought. The opportunity of a lifetime had just presented itself. Rang the Odd Job Man's mobile and invited him out for a fish dinner, if he wasn't doing anything. He said he'd love to come. I then rang the elegant new fish restaurant and made an early booking.

Sunday

Oh night of great triumph. Oh joy to the world. Oh heavenly turn of events. At last things are going my way.

The Odd Job Man looked really cool when he turned up. I was quite surprised. He had on a really nice suit with a red carnation in the buttonhole, which looked quite spunky. He brought me an orchid, which I thought was a bit old-fashioned, but it was a nice thought. He told me his father had always bought flowers for his mother. Decided to wear it. Looked interesting on my black dress, in a sort of thirties way.

I was a tad nervous about being seen by anyone from school, but I was pretty safe as this was a bit upmarket for the teachers of St Augustine's, whose usual idea of a night out was the 'all you could eat' smorgasbord at the local pub. Managed to get a table for two not far from the restaurant foyer. Nearby was a table set for twenty people. Perfect. I made sure we ordered the meal as soon as we could.

The slut from the Rhine arrived first, with Jamie in tow, and went to inspect her table. She took a couple of steps toward it and then she laid eyes on moi, just as the large plate of crustaceans landed at our table. The timing could not have been more perfect. She took one look and knew I had her by the short and curlies. Oh glorious triumph. She stared in horror as I threw up my hands in astonishment and said loudly, 'Oh my gooood, this is amazing. How are we ever going to get through all this? It'll take days.' With that, the slut grabbed Jamie's arm and they beat a hasty retreat.

In the foyer their guests were beginning to arrive. Dana waltzed in on John's arm. He'd obviously been given a leave of absence for the night.

A conference ensued. Meantime the Odd Job Man (who

fortunately had his back to the circus going on outside) and I were having a great time with the seafood, crab juice flying everywhere. Lucky we had those large serviettes tied around our necks.

Twenty people had now gathered in the foyer, all looking our way. The glass door opened and Dana came in. She marched up to the table. 'What are you doing here?' she demanded.

'Excuse me?' I said innocently. 'Oh, Jack. This used to be my best friend Dana.'

Dana looked at the Odd Job Man and literally went to water. He flashed a winning smile at her and I could see her legs turn to jelly. She became quite girlie. 'Oh. Pleased to meet you, Jack,' she simpered.

The Odd Job Man looked at me and said, 'Should I be pleased to meet her or not?'

'Well, it's a tough call,' I said. 'She hasn't been very nice to me of late.'

'Excuse me,' Dana hissed in my direction. 'Why are you talking about me when I'm standing right here? You're doing this on purpose, aren't you?'

'Doing what?'

'You knew we were coming here tonight. I said the new fish restaurant, didn't I?'

'Oh,' I said innocently, 'I thought you meant the one on the other side of town.'

'You knew exactly which one I meant,' she said tightly.

'Oh well,' I said, 'put it down to an honest mistake. Everyone makes them.'

'Well, you'll just have to leave,' she said.

'Oh, I don't think so,' I said. 'I believe we are entitled to finish our meal. Maybe you should check that point out with Lorelei.'

Dana looked at the Odd Job Man, smiled in that girlie

way, then beckoned me aside. 'Could we speak in private?' I got up from the table. She whispered in my ear, 'How about I ask the garbageman about his castle in Ireland and all the bullshit you've been telling everyone about him? And how you're using him to get Jamie back. How do you think that would go down?'

I whispered back: 'And how about I ring John's wife and tell her where he is tonight? How do you think that would go down?'

Dana was stymied and she knew it. 'You'll get yours,' she snarled.

'Hopefully I will,' I said. 'Tonight. Isn't he gorgeous?'

Dana looked at the Odd Job Man. Her legs went all wobbly again. She lurched out of the restaurant into the foyer where the agitated and furious slut from the Rhine was pacing.

'Problem?' said the Odd Job Man.

'She's a little mentally disturbed,' I said. 'Don't worry about it.'

At that moment I saw Larry had arrived. Lorelei was pointing at me and gesticulating wildly. He shrugged and looked very reluctant. She eventually pushed him through the foyer door and he headed over.

'Maggs,' he cried, kissing me on both cheeks before turning to the Odd Job Man. 'And Jaaaack, how lovely to seeeee you again.' Sizing him up and down. 'I just love that carnation.'

And that was as much as he managed to say. He just stood there staring at Jack, his right hip jigging, drool forming on his bottom lip. Drip, drip, drip on the Italian tiled floor.

'Larry,' I whispered, 'you're dribbling.'

'Oh am I?' he said. 'Sorry. Well I'd better get back. Enjoy your dinner. Nice to see you both.' And he left.

An argument ensued outside, with Larry shrugging and

Lorelei frothing at the mouth. Then came the moment I had waited for. In my peripheral vision, I could see that Jamie was heading over to our table. It was at that point that I leaned over and took the Odd Job Man's hand and gazed into his eyes. 'This is so nice,' I said. 'I'm really enjoying myself.'

I leaned across and kissed him on the mouth. He returned the kiss, obviously enjoying it. Perfect timing. Jamie arrived at the table.

'Margaret,' he said, 'could I have a word?' That pissed me off more than I can say. Calling me Margaret, just like that. What happened to Maggs, or Maggie, those wonderful terms of endearment he used to use?

I pretended I didn't hear him and kept kissing the Odd Job Man. Tongues were involved this time. Actually, now I think about it, I was highly turned on.

I then turned to Jamie and acted surprised. 'Oh, Jamie,' I said. 'I didn't see you there. Jack, this is Jamie. An old friend.'

Jack put out his hand to shake Jamie's, but Jamie ignored it. It was a good sign, I thought. Oh yes. Jealousy was written all over his face.

'Could I speak to you for a moment – in private?'

'But of course,' I said magnanimously. 'Would you excuse me, Jack, for just a minute?' I then moved away from the table with Jamie.

At this point my plan was that Jamie would fall at my feet, begging to come back to me because he could not stand – nay, could no longer live – now that he had seen another man's lips touch mine. He would ask for my hand in marriage, then promptly walk back to Lorelei and tell her the wedding was off before sending everyone home. Lorelei would be furious, of course, and vengeful. She would no doubt stalk me, make obscene phone calls . . . But it didn't happen quite like that, although I felt all the signs were there. Jamie was certainly pissed off.

'Margaret,' he said, 'as you can see, there are twenty people in the foyer waiting to come in. Lorelei is very upset. I'm thinking of you now. I don't want you to have to go back to court and be humiliated again.'

'Oh, I won't be going back to court,' I said. 'I haven't broken the conditions of the AVO, as you well know. I am entitled to finish my meal. There is absolutely nothing to stop you and the trollop and guests sitting down to dinner. I'm sure I won't be a bother.'

'Lorelei doesn't want to come in while you're here. She says you're too unpredictable. She doesn't trust you,' he said.

I smiled at him. 'Oh really? That's so silly. I would like to be her best friend. I think she's soooo interesting. But not to worry, we won't be long. Only another hour or so, and then we'll be gone.'

Jamie stood there like some big wet fish out of water, flapping and panting, gasping for air. I have to say it wasn't a good look. Then he went back outside.

I returned to the table. 'You're very popular this evening, Maggie,' he said, smiling. 'What have you done to deserve this?'

'It's just a personality trait,' I said. 'People are drawn to me.'

And now, serendipity. It was just one of those amazing events that happen when you're in step with the world, when everything is going your way. I was concentrating on the splendid meal before me. I didn't even see Lorelei marching through the door, purple with rage. I had just reached forward to stab a small blue swimmer with my fork. Suddenly I heard Lorelei scream out, 'You bitch!' I spun around to see the slut from the Rhine about to lunge at me and, at that glorious moment, the crab launched itself into the air and, spinning like a frisbee, hit Lorelei in the chest, where it clung tenaciously to the elaborate beading on her cashmere top. She stared with horror at the appendage on her bosom and started ranting like a madwoman. 'My Armani, my Armani, get it off!' Of course I tried to help, but as I moved towards her, she backed away and fell over the wine stand behind her.

The restaurant was now in an uproar, waiters running everywhere. Jamie, Dana and assorted guests rushed in to help as Lorelei lay on the floor. Dana tried to detach the crab, but Lorelei was now mental and was pretending her arm was hurt. Jamie helped her up.

'You'll get yours, cunt,' she screamed at me, then ran to the toilet, the crab still attached. Dana followed her.

Jamie stood there looking at me. Couldn't quite read the expression on his face, but it seemed like gratitude to me. At last he'd seen his future wife's true colours. Lorelei had been unmasked in front of all and sundry for the vile person she is. I mean, it just goes to show – money doesn't buy class. Jamie turned away and went after Lorelei. I felt well pleased with myself.

'I'm so sorry, Jack,' I said. 'This is proving to be most annoying. Let's go somewhere else.' He signalled for the bill and we left.

Can't remember what we talked about as we walked along the river bank, but we started laughing about the crab fiasco and couldn't stop. He asked me what the deal was and why they had been trying to make us leave. I made up a story about how Lorelei and I went to school together and always hated each other's guts. Maybe I should have told him the truth, but it didn't seem important.

When we arrived home, he kissed me gently on the cheek, said goodnight and left.

What the fuck is going on? I was expecting wild, passionate sex. There is something really weird going on here. Not sure what it is. Unless he has the clap or something, or an outbreak of herpes. That is the only thing I can think of, but then we could have used a condom, or he could have just sucked me off. Forced to finger myself yet again.

Dana dropped in. She was in a huge flurry. 'You are in big trouble,' she said pointing at me as she came through the door. 'Big trouble indeed.'

'What for?' I said.

'The restaurant business,' she said dramatically.

'I never violated the restraining order. The slut from the Rhine approached me. She hasn't got a leg to stand on,' I said.

'It's not her leg that's the problem,' said Dana. 'It's her arm. It's broken. Plaster right up to her elbow. She's going to have to wear a sling for the wedding.'

I cracked up laughing, couldn't stop.

'It's no laughing matter,' said Dana. 'It's going to spoil the whole look. Think of the photos.'

'Maybe she should call it off then,' I shrieked, 'or wear gloves.'

'Well, take it from me,' she said, 'she's out to get you.'

'Oooh,' I said, 'I'm shaking in my boots. What's she going to do, burn my house down?'

'Just beware,' said Dana. 'You have been given fair warning.'

I kept on laughing.

'So, where's the garbageman?' she said.

'He left just a few minutes ago,' I lied. 'I am totally shagged.'

'He's not bad looking for a janitor, and you say he has a big dick,' she said. 'I mean, if you're only using him to try and get Jamie back, I thought that maybe when you've finished, I could have a go. Have you got his phone number? I don't suppose you've changed your mind about the casserole dishes for the kitchen tea?' Dana has absolutely no scruples at all.

I expect to hear from Jamie later today re his dropping Lorelei, and then we can make plans for our wedding. Rang Mum and said I was sick, couldn't come to lunch. Wanted to stay in to wait for Jamie's call.

2 pm. Jamie *still* hasn't rung. Wonder what the problem is? Checked the phone several times, in case it was out of order. Tempted to ring him, but I feel I need to be patient. He is probably trying to sort out the mess now, then he will rush into my arms.

4 pm. Still no call. What is he waiting for?

6 pm. Tried to ring Lorelei, but she's got a silent number now.

8 pm. Why won't the Odd Job Man shag me?

Monday

Called a rehearsal at lunchtime today. Ann wanted to run the fat girl and the anorexic through the songs. Shit. Neither of them can sing a note. It's a disaster. Ann suggested that maybe I should rethink the Amanda/Sheridan situation. They are still swearing that they weren't involved in the vodka business. I explained to Ann that those two little slags have been a thorn in my side all year and if I let them get away with one more thing, they will never learn from their mistakes. I will not have done my duty as a role model. Mind you, after hearing Brenda squeeze out 'One day my

Prince will come', I was almost willing to change my mind.

As Ann tried to coax them onto, or even vaguely near, the right notes, I and the other girls dragged out some costumes from the storeroom, obviously left over from a Shakespeare or something. Suited us perfectly, except that Brenda was too fat for anything. I suggested she take the dress home and have her mother alter it. Brenda looked at me like I was from another planet. I started to explain that some mothers made their children's clothes, but it was a concept she couldn't relate to. Susan the asthmatic had an attack from all the dust that had accumulated on the cossies and had to be sent to the sick bay. Amanda and Sheridan nowhere to be seen.

Trudy the moron came up with a very good design for the backdrop. I had no idea she had any talents at all. A large castle painted on one side of the canvas and a few village houses on the other, with the swineherd's cottage painted on the left-hand side so that the action could move from one side of the stage to the other, according to what was going on. Art department slut has provided some paint. What exactly was her relationship with the Odd Job Man? None of my business really . . .

Lucky I made it to my English class early after lunch. Written on the blackboard was 'MISS ANDERSON IS A TOTAL CUNT.' Nice. Rubbed it off before the girls arrived.

No call from Jamie. I am now getting concerned.

Tuesday

What the fuck is going on with Alison? Not only were there more scabs on her upper lip, but she had these ludicrous pink streaks in her grey hair. Unbelievable. She looked like some sort of mad tiger. I don't like it. Where will it all end?

'Sooooo,' she said, 'how is it going then, Margaret?' And before I had a chance to answer, she just rabbited on: 'Fine, fine,' she said, 'Any clues on the . . . ? No, no, of course not, that would be asking too much, wouldn't it? So, what's been happening? Not much. So what are you doing here? I need help with my problems. But you say that every week and we don't seem to be getting anywhere. Have you looked in your diary? I believe the answer is there. Oh yessiree Bob, I have looked in my diary and I can't see anything that would suggest the cause of my turmoil. Oh well, I suppose that's the way it goes, you can't win them all.' And then suddenly she stopped. Mad as a fucking hatter. Am I expected to pay for this?

She sat there staring at me once again, wasting my precious time, not speaking. At long last: 'So, any clues yet as to your behaviour patterns, Margaret?' she said, slowly and deliberately as one speaks when they know they are slurring their words and they're trying not to show it. And then I smelt it. The distinct odour of alcohol was permeating the air. Alison had been drinking. 'Any clues regarding the comundrun?' she said, then quickly corrected herself: 'Conundrum.' The woman was pissed, I realised. She was totally off her face.

In normal circumstances I might have told her about the restaurant business. I know she would have had a good laugh, but Alison's humour seemed to have deserted her. She appeared surly and aggressive. And she kept muttering to herself.

Then she asked me about my drinking problem. I mean, what a cheek. Here she was as high as a kite and attempting to point the finger at me. I told her that I had curbed my drinking to a great extent, and in fact was in total control of myself and filling my life with projects and plans for the future. Didn't tell her that those plans included getting Jamie back by fair means or foul. I would tell her when it was all over.

She regarded me quizzically. 'Really,' she said. 'Goooooood. Goooood.' Then she put her head down on her arms on the desk and nodded off. Unbelievable. I tiptoed out. Not sure I can hack another two sessions.

Wednesday

Major setback. Court case this morning re drunk driving charge. Told them at school I had to attend a funeral. Turned out to be my own. Lost my licence for a year and copped a $500 fine. Shit. Just as things were looking up.

Spent lunchtime painting the backdrop according to Trudy's design. After school the Odd Job Man helped us hang it up. Was hoping that maybe he might brush up against me with his hardness, or slip his hand into my knickers when no one was looking, but he didn't. It's really starting to piss me off. It's not like we haven't shagged. He's seen me naked, for Christ's sake. Soooo horny. What *is* his problem? Don't I turn him on anymore? What is wrong with just good healthy sex, no strings attached?

We turned the lights on. Stage looks great.

Still no call from Jamie. Drove past his house. No car there. Maybe they're still trying to work out what to do with the presents.

Thursday

Wonders will never cease. Amanda and Sheridan turned up to drama club. Nice as pie, which makes me wonder what they're up to. 'We'd like to help, Miss,' they said. 'We want to prove to you that we're ready to work as part of the team.'

Not sure about this. I wouldn't trust those two as far as I could kick them. However, we need as much help as we can get. They will make up part of the crowd scene.

Everyone put their costumes on (Brenda's mother had obviously not had a chance to alter her dress – couldn't do the zip up) and we went through the last scene.

PRINCESS: But you're a swineherd? How can that be? How can I fall in love with someone so lowly?

SWINEHERD: How did I fall in love with someone so far above my station in life? Things happen that you don't plan on.

PRINCESS: So what do we do now?

SWINEHERD: Will you marry me?

PRINCESS: Oh yes. I want to live the rest of my life with you. We can have a lovely time in my castle.

SWINEHERD: But who will look after my pigs?

PRINCESS: We could have them at the wedding feast. On a spit.

SWINEHERD: What?

PRINCESS: Only kidding. See? I have learned to make jokes already.

SWINEHERD: We have to find a way to make this work. How are we going to do it? How are we going to live happily ever after?

(*Ask children in the audience for suggestions, then:*)

PRINCESS: I know. What if we were to live half the time at the castle and half the time with the pigs?

SWINEHERD: And would you like that, my darling? Living with the pigs?

PRINCESS: With you by my side, my love, it would be like living in paradise.

Amanda and Sheridan hit the deck at that. 'What a crock,' chortled Amanda. 'As if,' screamed Sheridan. Secretly I had to agree with them, but I didn't say anything.

Brenda became very defensive. 'Love does conquer all,' she said. 'That's what I think the play is all about.'

'Yeah but it's a load of bat shit,' screamed Amanda. 'Would you go and live in a pigpen with some swineherd?'

'If I was in love, I probably would,' said the fat girl.

'Oh yeah, right,' said Sheridan. 'Maybe if he had a big cock,' she screamed. 'Then you'd follow him anywhere.' She is so gross, that girl. Sent her out for five minutes.

Brenda and Wendy sang the final duet. It was truly awful.

I could hear Sheridan outside singing along with them. One of the few things their slag mothers did for them was to drag them along to Johnny's Talent School, to get what they considered to be the basics in life – singing and tap dancing. I have to admit Sheridan has a great voice. It could have been a huge finale – now we are stuck with Fat and Skinny. At that moment I was torn. But I felt that the life lesson they would learn from this experience would always stand them in good stead. Maybe the larde-arse and the skeleton would fall desperately ill and die of the plague or something. That is the only thing I can hope for.

Still no word from Jamie. I'll ask Larry over Friday, see what the score is.

Message from OJM – would I like to come to his place for dinner on Saturday? Not doing anything. Might as well . . . Hmm, starting to feel horny again. I will find a moment during the evening to sit on his cock. Don't think that's too much to ask. Cat meowing for his dinner. He's so demanding.

Friday

I am stunned. Larry says the wedding is still going ahead. What is going on? Surely Jamie has now seen, at first hand, what a stupid woman he is marrying? The way she so humiliated herself at the restaurant surely would have been the last straw. Why is he leaving it so late to call it all off? Maybe he just doesn't know how to say it. Maybe he hasn't got the courage. Mind you, it didn't take him long to tell me I was shafted.

Decided to draw Larry out on the subject. Asked him what he thought about the match. He said he thought it was as good as any he'd seen. They both seemed to be in love.

'But she's a moron,' I cried, 'the marriage will be a disaster.'

Larry was a bit taken aback. 'You're not still in love with Jamie, are you?' he said.

'Of course not,' I lied.

'Good,' he said. 'Jack is so much nicer, I think.'

I tried to hide my bitter disappointment. Only two weeks to go. Oh god. I am running out of time.

'Now,' he said, 'Christopher is about to start making the cake for the buck's night. Have you organised your friend to leap out? It will be such a hoot,' he said.

Of course. The buck's night. I'd almost forgotten. This is it, my one last chance to show Jamie how much I love him, how gorgeous I am, and to turn him away forever from the Rhine slut. This will be my great triumph. Slowly, ever so slowly rising with great majesty out of the cake, sugar coated, cream filled, Jamie unable to control his desire, me naked as the day I was born, with a few nicely placed rhinestones. He will lift me up and carry me home, and make mad passionate love to me. Then he'll realise he can't live without me and finally, FINALLY call off the wedding.

Larry showed me a sketch of the cake. 'Can I meet the girl soon?' he said. 'She will have to know exactly what to do. I want it to be just like Debbie Reynolds in *Singin' in the Rain*.'

Debbie Reynolds? I don't remember her being a raunchy chick . . . I bullshitted on how this girl – ah, Caroline – would be coming down from the country at the last minute, so he would have to give me all the instructions. The buck's night is next Friday.

Saturday

Got out *Singin' in the Rain* from the video shop. It's putrid. Debbie Reynolds is wearing this stupid pink bathing suit-type costume with a frill around the bottom, some chiffon hanging off one shoulder and a stupid side pocket thing that sticks out and holds streamers in it, which she then throws to the crowd. And to top it off, this stupid pink bathing hat. Unbelievable. There is no cream or icing sugar to be seen anywhere. She just comes out of a cardboard cake and does a pathetic dance, singing that crappy song my grandma used to sing, 'All I do is dream of you'. I don't think so.

Rang Larry. He screamed down the phone, 'Isn't it *wonderful*? It is soooo camp.'

'But I thought she would be naked,' I said, 'or sexy or something. I mean, I'm just asking for my friend.'

'Oh no,' said Larry, 'I want it to be tasteful and funny. It's a homage to Deb. Don't you remember how Jamie used to love her?'

Have to admit it was the one thing that I could never understand about Jamie. I mean, Debbie Reynolds? Gross. So, I'm not doing that. I'm not coming out of a stupid cardboard cake in that crappy outfit. I'm not making a fool of myself for anyone. I'll call Larry back and tell him Caroline has just died. Although, now that I think about it, once I'm inside that cake I can do what I like. I can wear what I like. No one will know until I rise up triumphant . . .

Midnight. OJM offered to pick me up, but I said I would get a cab. (Just in case the evening was boring and I could go home without having to rely on a lift.) Feeling extremely horny. I am going to have to insist on shagging him tonight. I can't just keep changing my knickers.

Arrived at the OJM's address. It was as I expected, one of those boring square blocks of cream brick flats, built in the fifties in a very boring street in the suburbs. He apologised for his meagre accommodation and ushered me inside. The décor in his flat was also as expected. Hired furniture of little taste, and no paintings or objets d'art to speak of. At least it was clean. He'd set the laminex table with napkins and candles and there were some flowers in a small jar.

He poured me some wine and went back to the stove. I imagined he would be cooking an Irish stew, or cabbage and potatoes, but in fact it was osso bucco, one of my favourites. I was a tad surprised. Never thought that the Odd Job Man would have any culinary expertise. I offered to help and he asked me to chop the parsley if I wanted to. Which I did. It was sort of nice, I have to say. There is something about cooking with someone that is very... intimate. Once again I was hoping for his hand to slip up my very short skirt, or his raging beast to push into my buttocks, at which point he'd bend me over the kitchen sink and fuck me stupid. But it was not to be. I mean, I did notice from time to time there was some movement at the station – Gigantor awakening – but he never made a move on me.

We talked about a lot of things. Apparently he'd been engaged once, but it didn't work out. I mentioned that I'd had a relationship that fizzled too, but didn't say much more. We laughed a lot about silly things. And that was it. He drove me home, walked me to the front door, said goodnight and disappeared. I mean, what the fuck is going on here? Have I lost my sex appeal? I had hoped when we reached the front door that he would drop to his knees, pull down my knickers and plunge his tongue into my wetness. But not even a lick.

Sunday

Went to Mum and Dad's for lunch. Sister and brother-in-law/kids there. The moron said he'd run into Patty and Graeme and they'd mentioned the caravan disaster. He suggested I might have been down there, hinted that I could have tampered with the taps. I denied it, of course. Said I hadn't been near the place. He then produced a jumper that I must have dropped in my haste to depart. Shit. It was one of my favourites and cost me a fortune. Moron said he would use it to polish his car if it didn't belong to anyone. What an arsehole. He knew damn well it was mine. He asked again re the pressure cooker. Shit. I keep forgetting. So much else on my mind.

Lunch was tripe in white sauce – either that or Gran's old elastic bandages. Dad thought it was sensational and just like his mother used to make, which made me wonder even more about my heritage. I said I was dieting. Made a peanut butter sandwich.

After lunch I went out to the shed to talk to my wise old dad. Wanted to ask his advice about the nature of love, what his views on relationships were. Mum and Dad had been together for a good thirty years. He must have some clues. Asked him what attracted him to my mother in the first instance.

He thought about that carefully. 'Sex,' he finally said. 'She was so hot, I couldn't wait to get my hands on her.'

I was totally revolted. I made some excuse to leave. I mean, what is wrong with this world? It's all topsy-turvy. Everyone wanting sex sex sex all the time. Even your parents.

Cat curled up on my knee. I'm so horny I could die.

Monday

Odd Job Man not parked in my spot. Wonders will never cease. His car was down the other end of the parking area. I cannot work him out. There's something weird going on here.

Ann took Brenda and Wendy for a special singing rehearsal at lunchtime. Pathetic. I took the others for some crowd scene rehearsals. Sheridan and Amanda being most helpful. They are up to something, I know.

Problem with the sound. The Odd Job Man came in. He

had to rewire the speaker system. Seems to be able to do most things. There is something quite fascinating about watching a man fix things.

Amanda sidled up to me. 'Pretty good with his hands, eh, miss? Bet he could hotwire anything.' She is such a slut.

He finished the wiring and left. I had this odd feeling about him. Can't put my finger on it. Maybe that's the problem. I am masturbating myself into an early grave. Then I saw him talking to the art slut Pamela Goodwin. Really pissed me off. They were laughing together. What is that all about? And more to the point, why is it annoying me?

After school I went to a party shop and bought a whole bag of stuff. Had a totally brilliant idea with regard to the buck's night. Know exactly what I am going to do. Bought a G-string, some rhinestones and some glue and glitter. I have it all planned now. I will dress up in the stupid bathing suit and have everything else underneath. Once I am in the cake, I will slip the Debbie Reynolds outfit off and spring almost naked into Jamie's arms. This is a do or die effort now. My appearance at the buck's night has to tip Jamie over the edge.

Made the cossie. Had some problems with the rhinestones, which I stuck to my nipples with glue. Couldn't get them off. Spent a good hour trying to sponge them, but to no avail. Had to use methylated spirits in the end. Now I have sore tits. Must be a trick to it. Those follies girls seemed to manage. Will just have to put glitter over my body from head to foot.

Bored. Maybe I should ring the Odd Job Man. Pretend I have a problem re the lighting/sound for the panto. Maybe his herpes has cleared up by now . . . He's coming over.

Put on my tightest skirt, my skimpiest jumper. Did a lot of reaching for things like tea canisters, cups etc., so that my breasts would show a little from underneath the jumper.

He never made a move. He did say something weird though. He grinned and asked me the real reason for inviting him over. He suggested there was in fact no problem with the lighting/sound at all. Everything was ready to go. Was it because I enjoyed his company? I mean, what a fucking cheek. Who does he think he is? As it turned out, however, he was fairly entertaining and cracked a few jokes which kept me amused.

Then, stupidly, it was out of my mouth before I could stop myself. I asked him what his relationship with Pamela Goodwin was. He laughed. 'You're not jealous, are you?'

Unbelievable. I was appalled. Said it was the most ridiculous thing I had ever heard. Why on earth would I be jealous? Said I was just asking because I wouldn't want her to think that there was anything going on between us and cause a problem if in fact they were . . . in a relationship. He laughed again. Couldn't stop. Then he said he had to go. Had to be at school early as it was bin day. For some reason I was really annoyed.

Mind you, this time at the door, he kissed me very gently on the mouth and just for the briefest moment let his tongue caress mine. This is only making me hornier. And he never answered the question re the art slut. That really pissed me off.

2 am. Tossing and turning. Something is really irritating me about this whole Odd Job Man thing.

Tuesday

Miss McConnichy said she would drop in and look at a rehearsal tomorrow. She wants to make sure the panto is suitable for primary school children. No smut, etc. I mean, here's a woman whose morals are extremely questionable talking about protecting the minds of young children. I started to wonder when Miss McConnichy knew she was a dyke. Did she ever try on her father's suits? Or shave? Or try to stand up while she was peeing? Why am I thinking this shit? I am totally distracted at the moment, having a lot of weird thoughts.

Another outrageous session with Alison. Smell of alcohol apparent again. More scabs on the upper lip and more pink streaks in the hair. And she'd plucked her eyebrows. All of them. Just thin pencil lines drawn on her bare brow. And instead of sitting there staring at me, she launched straight in: 'I am sick and tired of you turning up week after week looking for the answer when it is right there in front of you.' I was stunned. I mean, fancy speaking to a patient like that.

'Do you have the diary with you?' she said. I was about to say it was in my bag when she swooped like a hawk, grabbed my bag and pulled out the diary. She was like a woman possessed.

She started banging the diary on the desk. 'Pick a page, any page,' she said. 'It's all in there!' She was becoming a little unhinged at this point. 'I don't even have to read it. I know what's there. Me, me, me, me, me me me!' she ranted, now on the verge of hysteria. She opened a page and thrust it in my face. 'Read it,' she said.

'I don't want to read it,' I whimpered.

'All right,' she said, 'I'll read it to you. Let's see . . . you are the most selfish, self-centred, egocentric, self-absorbed, pompous, conceited, stuck-up snob I've ever known.' Of all the pages in the diary, Alison had to pick that one.

'It was a joke,' I said. 'Dad was only joking when he said that.'

'Oh,' she said, 'your father said that, did he? It's no joke, Margaret. It's true. Let's pick another one, shall we?' She kept flipping through the pages. 'Look, look,' she ranted. 'Look how you denigrate people all the time . . . the lesbian . . . the Rhine slut, fat and skinny, the moron . . . the Odd Job Man – don't they have names?'

'Tell me,' she said, now out of her chair and looming in front of me like Frankenstein's monster. 'Do you care about anyone but yourself? Do you ever, for one moment, think about other people's feelings?'

At that point I lost my cool. 'I am not here to find out about other people's feelings. I'm here to find out about mine! I'm the one whose emotions have been crushed and shattered and turned into nanny goat's shit by all and sundry. Why should I give a rat's arse how other people feel?' Then I tried to grab my diary. I was concerned she might read the stuff about herself. A tussle ensued, a bit of pushing and shoving.

'Let go, Alison,' I cried. 'This is my property, you have no right to read it.'

'I am trying to help you,' she said, unwilling to let go.

I wrestled the diary from her. She staggered backwards, falling into her chair. 'You know something? You're the problem here,' I said, pointing at her. 'You call yourself a psychologist. You're the one who needs help. That fall on the head has given you brain damage – and maybe you should get some hormones or something. You are totally out of control.'

She sat there staring after me as I ran out the door.

Outside I hailed a taxi. I could barely contain myself. I mean, what a thing to say, did I ever think about anyone else's feelings? What an outrage. If I wasn't concerned about Jamie's feelings I would never consider trying to break up his relationship with the slut. It is only because I believe he would be far happier with me than with Lorelei that I am continuing with my attempts to sabotage the wedding plans. It's clearly for unselfish reasons. A truly heroic quest.

And my sister, for example – if I wasn't thinking about her, I would never try and point out what a moron her husband is. The kids at school . . . I'm not just doing the panto to retain my employment, I think about them too and how they are advancing their god-given talents . . . well, I would if they had any. And I've been tough on Amanda and Sheridan, sure, but that's only been to show them the way. I am trying to be a good role model.

And Aunt Pen . . . well, that's her problem, not mine. And the Odd Job Man: now there's an example of my amazing goodness. The fact that I have even been out with him at all shows I am not a selfish snob. Okay, I am using him, but he's getting something out of it, I'm sure. There are so many examples of my caring about other people. No, Alison has the wrong end of the stick here. I am not sure I can hack another session with her.

Wednesday

Larry around after school. Drill about the buck's night. My friend Caroline would go with his mate Christopher to the Grosvenor Hotel where the buck's night was being held. The cake would then be stored in the staff cloakroom, on a baggage trolley. At the specified time a member of the Grosvenor's staff would collect the trolley with the cake on it and take it to the private room where the buck's night was being held.

Larry then unwrapped the costume, which was an exact replica of the crappy pink one in the movie. He'd made it himself. He was so proud of it. He insisted I try it on, seeing as I'd said I was the same size as Caroline.

I put the outfit on. Larry thought I looked adorable. He then insisted on coaching me so I could in turn coach Caroline. 'The arms held so,' he said, demonstrating, 'then climb out of the cake, throw the streamers around, bow, wave and run off.' Larry said he would have loved the song as well, but without rehearsal it would be asking too much. Poor Larry. If only he knew what I was really going to do.

He gave me a big kiss and left. I feel a bit awful. Larry is so sincere and such a sweet, generous person. But I'm sure when he witnesses Jamie's passion for me, and the happiness that will flow from this event, I'm sure he'll forgive me for not doing his bidding to the letter.

Suddenly feel very flat. Everything is in place for this final assault, which I believe absolutely will alter the course of my life forever. So what is my problem? I should be excited.

Rang the Odd Job Man. Not sure why. Just wanted a chat, I suppose. Made up an excuse that I was a bit worried about the run-through of the panto tomorrow. He was very nice and said he was sure it would be fine.

I was hoping he might say that he would come over, but he didn't. Am going to end up with RSI if I keep tapping my twat the way I do.

Thursday

Full run-through of the panto. Miss McConnichy in to watch. Fat and Skinny were truly terrible. They fluffed their lines, their singing was atrocious. The lard-arse tripped and fell at one stage, although I did notice she was near Sheridan at the time, and that Sheridan just happened to have her foot out, but in fact her fall was the only entertaining thing in the whole show. Amanda and Sheridan pissed themselves laughing. It was a total disaster.

Miss McConnichy not impressed but, as I explained to her, it was the first full run-through and we had a week and a half to get it right. She asked why Amanda and Sheridan weren't playing the leads as they can both sing and dance, and it was her belief that in fact they had originally been cast in those roles. Certainly that was their parents' understanding.

She was hedging towards yet more blackmail, but I stood my ground. Bullshitted on about how important I thought it was to give a chance to those students who otherwise might not get a go. Suggested that it had given Brenda and Wendy more confidence in themselves, which was not, I have to say, apparent in their appalling performances, but I argued that it was character-building and stretching their limits. It was certainly stretching mine. I knew I was up shit creek. Miss McConnichy was not convinced. However, I said that I planned to stay back after school every night and work with them.

I am dog meat. There is no way those two slugs are going to get it together by Tuesday week. Worked with them after school. Just remembering their lines is a major trial and walking and talking at the same time is not within their range of capabilities. I am a rat on a sinking ship.

OJM came in to sweep up the hall. I was pretty dejected. He sat down next to me. Didn't talk for a while, but for some reason I felt a little better. I explained the situation re the hopelessness of my cast. I talked about A and S, how they would have been perfect if not for the vodka incident. The Odd Job Man then dropped a bombshell. He said that they had not tampered with the fruit punch. It was two boys from St Andrew's. He'd seen them stash the vodka earlier, but thought it was just for their own use. Didn't know that A and S had been blamed.

My heart lifted when I heard that. Thought I would be able to dump Fat and Skinny and give A and S back the roles. But realised I couldn't. I have come unstuck on this. After my big speech to Miss McConnichy re giving those two girls a chance, I cannot go back on my word. I would look like a total jerk.

OJM offered to drive me home. Told him about my dilemma. He agreed. Said that it was too late to dump Brenda and Wendy. Said it showed what moral fortitude I had. He suggested that nevertheless I could still apologise to Amanda and Sheridan re the accusation. No way I'm ever going to do that. It would give them the upper hand.

OJM is turning out to be quite a nice person. What a pity he's a janitor. He stayed till quite late, we talked about lots of things. Once again laughed a lot. As he was leaving, he kissed me on the mouth, lingering slightly. I was totally thrown by the feelings that it gave me. He asked me whether I was free tomorrow night. I said no. Funny, I wished I was. But of course I have the buck's night.

Friday

Tempted to come clean to Amanda and Sheridan. On yard duty, however, I caught them smoking in the toilets. Decided not to apologise to them. Gave them detention instead.

Tonight is the night. This is it. At last I will have Jamie back. It is what I have worked for, what I have planned. Later tonight we will lie in each other's arms and rue the time we have wasted. Time that we can never make up. We will whisper sweet nothings and pledge our love forever and ever. So what is this odd feeling I have in the pit of my stomach? Maybe nerves. Something not quite right. Is there anything I have forgotten? And where am I going to hide the glitter?

11 pm. Need to write everything down. Not sure what has happened. Am in a state of shock. It's not what I expected but I think my life has changed forever.

Christopher arrived on time. The cake, an exact replica of the Debbie Reynolds cake, was in the back of his van. I introduced myself as Caroline and we headed to the Grosvenor Hotel. Christopher, who was obviously another sausage jockey, rabbited on about the cake, how thrilled he was with it. It was made of balsawood but, with the addition of the plaster of Paris 'cream', it was perhaps a little heavier than he'd hoped. It would take the two of us to lift it.

We carried the cake, covered in a sheet, through the crowded foyer into the staff cloakroom as prearranged. The cake was placed on a trolley. With my G-string underneath, I changed into my Debbie Reynolds outfit with the stupid hat, just as Jeremy, the staff member who had been briefed on the proceedings, came in. He stared at me. 'Debbie Reynolds,' he screamed. 'Oh my god, what a hoot!'

Christopher and Jeremy lifted the cake and I climbed underneath. Christopher, who had a hot date and couldn't wait, wished me good luck and left.

The space was smaller than I expected. And it was dark. Not much light was coming in through the paper top that I was to break out of.

At that moment disaster struck. The manager came in and told Jeremy he was needed urgently. There was a problem at one of the private functions. Some footballers had gone berserk and were tearing the place up. Jeremy tapped on the cake. 'Back in a minute, Deb,' he said, and he was gone.

Suddenly alone, I now had the time I needed to take off the pink suit. Only it was impossible. I could not move an inch. And the more I struggled, the more stuck I became. And then I realised that the vial of glitter paste which I had secreted in my G-string had lost its cap. And what with the heat from my body and my efforts to get out of the pink suit, the paste was heading south where it wasn't meant to go. I was in agony.

It was getting hotter by the minute. Stuck in that crouched position in that awful dark space, I felt like I was back in the womb. I could barely breathe. Had Christopher remembered to put in airholes? I started to feel dizzy and faint. My life with Jamie suddenly flashed before my eyes. Jamie, Jamie, Jamie, where did it all start to go wrong? It couldn't just have been the last argument. It must have been something else. What did I do? What was it I said?

And he wasn't perfect either. I mean, there were times when he drove me nuts – forgetting to put the rubbish out (how odd to think of rubbish at a time like this), and leaving the toilet seat up. Dropping his clothes everywhere. And what had happened to the exciting things we used to do? When did he last take me on a wild drive through the suburbs, or shag me in a boiler room, or cook for me and look after me when I was drunk and disorderly? He was too busy with his mates or watching the football or drinking down the pub. And what if it was true about the poems? Did we ever really have anything in common? And why had he never asked me to marry him?

And then it happened in that darkest of places. An epiphany. The scales fell from my eyes, like Paul on the road to Damascus. I don't really love Jamie at all. I am . . . I am . . . I am in love with the Odd Job Man.

Oh my god. Oh, what a revelation to hit me at that particular moment. Why couldn't it have been earlier? All this time, slowly creeping up on me, the Odd Job Man had inveigled his way into my mind, into my life. He had cleverly played me with his large member to gain my attention, then bit by bit his arrogance, his charm, his wit, and, dare I say, his kindness had sucked me in. It was all so clear now. I had to get out. I had to escape. I had to find Jack and tell him how much I loved him.

I tried lifting the cake, but it was too heavy. I was trapped like a rat. And at that moment, the door opened and another staff member came in. 'Sorry to keep you. Jeremy is held up. Taking you now.' And the trolley began to move.

I called out, but there was so much noise in the foyer what with a piano-player and guest chatter that I couldn't be heard. The roller-coaster was now reaching the crest of the hill and was about to come off the rails and head over the precipice.

There was the sound of a door opening and closing and I hoped by some amazing turn of events I was now alone in another storeroom. But it was not to be. As I jettisoned myself out of the cake gasping for air, there before me, as far as the eye could see, all dressed in stripy shirts, were drunk and disorderly rugby players. Oh terrible blunder. I had been delivered to the wrong room.

For several seconds they stood staring at me in my little pink outfit. I stared back at them. Nothing was said. Maybe, I thought to myself, if I just said, 'Oops, sorry – wrong room,' they might let me out. But nor was this to be. Suddenly the whooping began. In unison they yelled, 'Get it off, get it off, get it off.' Like animals, they advanced towards the cake, banging their fists on the plaster of Paris which, like my life, was crumbling all around me. I had visions of being torn apart, of terrible orgies at my expense. The mob descended on me and just as I was about to be dragged out of the cake, a voice yelled from somewhere towards the back of the room: 'Just a minute!'

All went quiet. The crowd parted and a large Maori winger moved forward, pointing his enormous finger at me. I stood there trembling. It was not too long ago that Maoris were cannibals, I remembered. They used to eat their enemy's liver. Was I now to be part of a rugby hangi?

He came right up to me and stared at me. And then he spoke, his deep voice resonating throughout the room: 'Debbie Reynolds,' he cried. 'It's Debbie Reynolds from *Singin' in the Rain*.' A great cheer went up from the mob. Then, with the Maori winger leading, they all began to sing: 'Singin' in the rain, just singin' in the rain, what a glorious feeling I'm happy again . . .'

They all began swaying in time, holding their mugs of beer aloft. I saw a chance and I took it. I climbed out of the cake and tap danced as fast as I could towards the door, singing along with them. I was out the door before they realised I had escaped.

In the foyer I ran into Larry. He was looking for the cake. He was stunned to see me. I told him that Caroline had been caught up and I'd taken her place. Told him about the delivery to the wrong room. Poor Larry. He was devastated.

Got dressed and caught a cab home. Just out of the bath now. Have rung the Odd Job Man. Told him it's an emergency. He's on his way over. Hope I've got all the glitter out of my crack.

Saturday

Oh joy, oh wonder, oh delirious love abounding. I cannot believe how much in love I am. I am laughing, I am over the moon, bells are ringing. When Jack arrived, I opened the front door and he said, 'What's happened?'

I said, 'I think . . . I think . . . I think I'm in love with you.' He looked at me and started to laugh. Said he'd loved me from the first moment he saw me. Thought I was funny, honest, not afraid to say what was on my mind, had integrity. Qualities he's always admired. He didn't want any bullshit. He wanted me to come to him when I was ready, when the time was right. And now it was. He then lifted me up and carried me into the bedroom. We made mad passionate love all night long. Oh glorious night. He left this morning to change his clothes and is coming back in an hour or so.

Oh magical world. That I could be so lucky. As I lay in his arms last night after our passion had abated for the fourth time, I had time to consider some of the serious problems of this match. How am I going to introduce him to my friends, my family? This business of the 'garbageman' will not do at all. Have to think of another title – janitor is no good. Caretaker maybe, groundsman, something like that . . . I have seen him sweeping up the leaves and tending to the compost, though perhaps horticulturist would be going a little far. Suddenly occurred to me that maybe Jack had hidden talents, besides the obvious. Talents that could be encouraged, nurtured.

Started to muse on all sorts of amazing possibilities. Who knows? I mean, he is Irish after all. Think of the literary heritage: Joyce, Behan, Beckett – the list is endless. He could end up writing a Pulitzer Prize winner. I mean, why not? It's in the blood. They are practically born with a novel under their arm . . . or maybe he plays a musical instrument, like the fiddle or the harp. Or he could be a singer. Never heard of an Irishman who couldn't sing . . . Who knows, he could be a minefield of talent. I will, of course, encourage him to pursue any of these goals.

Oh wonderful life. This is going to be so amazing. We're off to the markets this afternoon to shop. And then a picnic. I'll buy some olives, get some crusty rolls, some ham and some red wine. Pretend we're in Tuscany. Then we'll make mad passionate love again. Wonder if I should take him to meet Mum and Dad tomorrow?

Sunday

Mum put on a 'special' lunch today. I thought in fact she'd gone for the rabbit, which might have been a homage to Jack's peasant heritage, but it turned out to be just a very dry chicken. Decided it would be good form to take Mum the pressure cooker at last. It would show Jack what a thoughtful daughter I was, and what a nice person. Mum was over the moon. She jammed all the vegies in and cooked them in five minutes flat, then served them as a mash. Jack was charming. Said how delicious it was. Mum went to water. Thought he was just gorgeous.

After lunch he went out into the shed with Dad and they talked about home brew, cars, men's stuff. He was quite a hit. I managed to hedge around what he did for a living. Just said I met him at school. Think they assumed he was a teacher of some sort. Mum asked Jack how long he was staying in Australia. Jack said he wasn't sure. His visa was almost up, but who knows? He might find a reason to stay. Then he looked at me in a meaningful way.

Was this a proposal? Oh god. He wants to marry me. Is this all too rushed? Hope I'm not on the rebound. I have never been happier in my life.

Monday

Practically floated into school. I am totally in the love bubble. Ignored some snide remarks from Amanda and Sheridan, who said I looked like I'd been shagged all weekend. I decided to rise above it.

Told Ann about Jack and me. She is the only one I can trust. Ann was thrilled. Said she thought it was a perfect match. She said she would keep the secret.

Took the rehearsal today with Brenda and Wendy. They sounded quite good, I thought, but as Ann kept wincing every time they opened their mouths, I decided maybe it was just my altered state of perception. Everything is bright and beautiful. The world is rosy. Even Amanda and Sheridan look fine in this light. I could forgive them almost anything. Somehow nothing matters any more. Of all the shit I've been through, I have now come out the other side. No thanks to Alison. In fact, now that I think about it, I don't need her anymore. I will cancel my session for tomorrow night.

Rang Alison at home. Her answer-phone was on. Left a message telling her that I had found true love and happiness, contrary to her expectations and advice, and that our sessions had been a complete waste of time and money. All that crap she was on about . . . repeating patterns, selfish behaviour, being a snob, destructive, obsessive, concentrating on self, it's all rubbish. All I needed was someone to come along and give me some unconditional love and attention.

Halfway through my diatribe I heard Alison pick up the phone. She didn't say anything, just breathed heavily at the other end. I could almost smell the scotch. I finished up by saying to her, 'And you want to know something else, Alison? You are in the wrong job!'

I heard her hang up the phone. Hope she wasn't offended. I was just trying to offer her some good advice, that's all.

I wonder if I should ask Jack to move in? I mean, Jamie and I moved in straightaway. Only this time it'll be forever. Must check out the adult education program, see what courses are available and suggest them to Jack.

Tuesday

Hardly any sleep. Made passionate love all night. I am totally immobilised by this amazing love. My snatch is throbbing endlessly. And still I want more. That giant member is a gift from heaven. Suggested that Jack move in. He said, why not? No point in putting off the inevitable.

Panto rehearsals. Brenda and Wendy still not cutting the mustard. They are trying hard, but they have absolutely no idea at all. Amanda and Sheridan skulking round. They are looking very pleased with themselves.

I am laughing so much I can scarcely put pen to paper. Dana dropped in after work. She raved about how wonderful the kitchen tea was in spite of the absence of my Corning ware. Lorelei was apparently overjoyed.

'Maybe you won't have to lick her arse for a while then,' I said.

'You are sooo nasty,' she said. 'And after what you've done to her.'

'I never broke her arm,' I said, 'she broke it herself.'

'That's not the way she sees it,' Dana said.

'Ooooh, scary,' I replied. 'Is she still going to burn my house down?'

'Let's just say she's waiting for the right opportunity. I am saying no more.'

Dana's real purpose in this visit, however, was to show off her bridesmaid's outfit. She insisted on modelling it for me, seeing as I would not be coming to the wedding. Not sure whether she was fishing or not. Maybe she thought I was going to try something to spoil the day. It is the furthest thing from my mind. True love has changed all that.

As she put the dress on, I took the opportunity to tell her about Jack moving in. 'The garbageman?' she shrieked. 'Are you serious?'

'Absolutely,' I said. 'It's true love. I have never been happier.'

'Really?' she said. She was stunned. 'So, have you told him about all that stuff you made up? About the castle and the gold mines? And how you were using him to get Jamie back?'

'I never made it up,' I lied. 'It's all true.'

'So you'll be going to live in the castle?' Dana queried.

'Definitely,' I replied. Maybe I should have come clean then, but I wanted to get right up her nose. 'We'll honeymoon in the Caribbean, though. Ireland can be very cold in the winter. And the castle is so draughty, apparently.'

'Really?' said Dana, adjusting her little sequinned hat. 'How very interesting.' She turned around. 'So what do you think?'

I have to admit the dress was gorgeous. Delicate fabric with sequins all over it.

'Can you imagine how much it cost?' gushed Dana. 'What a wonderful, generous person Lorelei is. And such a sweet, sweet nature . . .'

At that point George came in looking for his dinner. He started rolling on his back and attention seeking, doing cutsie-pie things.

Dana looked at him with disdain. 'It's really the ugliest cat I've ever –' And that's as far as she got. George darted forward, lifted his tail and sprayed all over her Collette Dinnigan. Dana's screams could be heard a mile away.

'Fucking arsehole,' she sobbed. 'I'll never get that stink out.' I could not speak for laughing. 'This is all your fault,' she screamed. 'You'll pay for this.' She grabbed her clothes and ran off.

Gave George an extra tin of tuna supreme for dinner.

Jack bringing a few things over tonight. Hope he doesn't have second thoughts. Could my life be any more perfect?

Wednesday

Please, let the ground open up and swallow me whole. Why didn't I see it coming? Dana warned me, but I never expected such havoc could be wreaked. Just when the world was at my feet, when life and harmony and all the good things had come my way. My life is totally shattered. My happiness crushed and ground into the bitumen. Where is Alison when I need her?

Went over to the primary school to ascertain the number of children coming for the performance next Tuesday, so we could set up the seating before the weekend. Staff and kids very excited. Headmistress of the primary school thought it was a wonderful gesture, the girls giving up their time to entertain the littlies. Praise heaped on my head also, for engendering the idea. Brief interlude with Jack in the hall, a stolen kiss, words of love and foreverness.

Had a spare period, so I went to talk to Ann. Told her that Jack was moving in on Saturday. She thought that was great. She is such a wonderful person. From the vantage point of the library, I looked for Jack in the school grounds. He was there, near the gates, sweeping the path. He looked amazing with his tee shirt clinging to his body.

My mind wandered back to last night in bed. After hours of making love, we talked about all the things that were important to both of us in the relationship – respect, honesty, loyalty, and truth at all times. We swore fidelity. Approached the subject of further education with him. He said basically he wasn't interested. Said he was happy with what he was doing, and asked if I had a problem with that. 'Oh no,' I lied, 'I love you for what you are.' Down the track, of course, I will suggest various directions he could take by way of a new career. We then made love again. It was a joy to discover that he gave great head. Oh bliss.

He must have felt me watching him. He looked up from the school grounds and smiled at me. My legs turned to jelly. We even have telepathic communication with each other.

And then I saw it. Oh, damned vision from hell. Like the ghost of Christmas past, a pale blue Audi sports car with slightly damaged duco had pulled up in front of the elaborate wrought-iron gates which bear the school motto 'Carpe diem'. To my horror I saw my ex best friend Dana at the wheel, with the one-armed slut from the Rhine beside her. Lorelei was about to lure my life onto the jagged rocks and leave me forever shipwrecked on that desert island of misery and heartache where single people go. She got out of the car and signalled to Jack, who walked across to her.

I ran out of the library, down the steps, out into the quadrangle and through the archway, but it was all too late. The die had been cast, the damage done. The car had gone by the time I arrived. There was no sign of Jack. I searched the school grounds, but he was nowhere to be seen. And his car was gone. How I managed to get through the rest of the day I have no idea.

Went around to his flat after school and knocked on the door. He wasn't home. Sat on the steps for three hours waiting for him. Eventually he arrived. I tried to kiss him. He stopped me.

'I wasn't using you,' I cried. 'Well, I was at first, but that's changed now that I love you. And the business about the castle and the gold mines and stuff, I was only kidding. I love you being a janitor. I think emptying the garbage is a great thing to do, and sweeping up the dirt. Well, I don't love it, but I'm sure there's always room for improvement. Look, we can work this out. Everyone makes mistakes. Don't throw this all away. I love you.' I stood there hoping he would take me in his arms and hold me and say wonderful, soothing, understanding things. But it was not to be.

He looked at me squarely. 'It could never work, Maggs. You know it and I know it. We're from different worlds. You could never be happy living with a janitor. You'd be wanting me to change all the time.'

'No,' I cried. 'I promise, I wouldn't. I'm really happy with you the way you are. I could change. We could start again.'

He looked at me. 'I've decided to go home,' he said. 'Back to Ireland. I'm heading out tomorrow night. My visa's up anyway. Sometimes it's best to put a distance on things,' he said. 'I'll run you home.'

We drove in silence. When we pulled up at my place, tears were running down my cheeks. He kissed me gently and I went inside.

My life is totally over. Can't sleep. Please let me wake up from this awful dream.

Thursday

Arrived at school early to see if I could find Jack. See if I could somehow talk him around. Maybe he'd change his mind.

The first person I ran into was Mr Hedges, the janitor who'd been away on long service leave. I asked where Jack was. 'He's left,' said Mr Hedges. 'Anything I can do, love?' he said.

My heart went cold. This cannot be happening. How am I going to get through the day?

Tried ringing Jack at home. Number is disconnected and he's not answering his mobile. Nothing I can do. Told Ann what had happened. She was sympathetic, but thought maybe I'd done the wrong thing. Suggested that I should go around to Jack's after school. Try again.

Jack was about to get into a taxi to go to the airport when I arrived. I burst into tears. He took me in his arms. 'Come on now, what's all this?' he said gently.

'I'm so sorry,' I sobbed. 'I'm so very sorry.'

'Me too,' he said. He kissed me on the lips and headed to the taxi.

'Will you be back?' I said.

He smiled. 'Maybe.'

And he was gone.

Midnight. Crying so hard I can't sleep. George licking my tears. The pain is so awful. Right. I'm going to get those two cunts if it's the last thing I do. I am going to totally fuck up that wedding!

2 am. Have come up with a plan.

Friday

Stayed at home today. Needed to work out my strategy. Can't believe everything went so badly. Just when I had the world at my feet. But Dana and Lorelei will feel the power of my wrath. They will wish they had never been born.

Rode down to the church to make sure of the layout, and have bought the necessary items to execute my devious scheme. A plastic container of premium grade motor oil and a large David Jones bag. Oh joy, oh great delight. I remembered the Blake poem as I cut the bottom corner off the plastic bag.

> *In the morning glad I see*
> *My foe outstretched beneath the tree.*

Double-checked everything. Time of wedding: 11 am. Church: St Aloysius. Time needed to cycle there: approximately twenty minutes. Ability to carry apparatus in bicycle basket: all fits perfectly. Where to position myself to view incident where I won't be seen: grassy knoll in park opposite church. This will need perfect timing, perfect precision. Checked and rechecked the layout. Steps leading up to the front door of the church: twelve, main doors opening out onto steps. Oh yes. I will have my revenge. Practised all day. Operation Spoil-the-wedding is on.

2 am. Oh, Jack, where are you? Please come back. I miss you so.

Saturday

Hiding under the bed. Someone banging on the door. Think it is Dana. She can get fucked. Pretend I'm not here. Why me? Why does everything I do turn to manure? Yet again the fates have conspired against me. Yet again somehow my perfect planning and precision has gone awry. And this time, I could be in very, very deep shit.

First thing to go wrong: flat tyre on the bike. By the time I arrived at the church, the doors were closed and everyone was inside. I could hear singing. I assumed the wedding had begun. Luck at this stage was on my side. No one around except an old drunk wrapped in a grubby doona, asleep beside the church steps.

I tethered my bike under a fig tree in the park and wandered nonchalantly across to the church as if I was vaguely interested in the architecture, checking out the gargoyles that leered down at me, watching my every move.

Could they have been trying to tell me something? Warn me, perhaps?

Undid the top of the container and let the oil trickle out of the plastic bag as I walked sideways across the steps, leaving a trail of slippery fluid behind me. Suddenly a voice called out to me: 'Hey girlie – you're leaking.'

I froze. It was the drunk. He'd woken up and was now watching me. I pretended not to hear him as I continued my lethal task, laying the snail trail across each of the steps. He called out again: 'Hey, girlie,' but soon lost interest and settled back in his doona.

Now the twelve steps were covered with oil. Once finished I went across to the park and dumped the empty bottle of oil in the rubbish bin. It was so easy. I was ecstatic. All was ready, set to go. I sat on the grassy knoll and waited for the show to begin. I checked the time. Service should nearly be over. I could hardly wait for the moment when Lorelei and Dana and assorted guests would skate across that icy surface and down the slippery dip – dresses all covered in oil and dirt. What havoc I would wreak. What joy. What a surprise they would get. And what wonderful photos for the album.

Looking back, maybe I should have noticed there was something amiss at the front of the church. There were, indeed, no wedding cars to be seen. None of the usual chauffeurs hanging about, fagging on. Just a large minibus. Perhaps if I had taken that information on board, I might have realised that no way would the slut from the Rhine entertain the idea of a community van to carry the wedding party to the reception. This fact in place, maybe I could have prevented the disaster that followed.

It was not until my mobile rang that I was alerted to the awful knowledge. It was Dana. She started screaming down the phone that thanks to me and my fucking cat, she had been dropped from the wedding party this morning because Lorelei kept gagging every time she came near the Collette Dinnigan. Of course it was all my fault. And now she had nothing to wear and demanded that she borrow my spotty dress and hat. It was at this point that my heart missed a beat. I asked her how come she wasn't inside the church. And then she told me – the wedding had been put back till two o'clock this afternoon to accommodate a special saint's day service.

Oh foul and spurious fate. Oh treachery of time . . . oh impending doom. What awful circumstances had led to this? What tragedy would follow? And, more to the point, who the fuck was in the church and who would head down that slippery slope? I was on the point of running across to warn the congregation, but it was too late.

Suddenly the doors were thrown open and out into that bright spring day a dozen young virgins in habits and veils, Brides of Christ, just married to Jesus and headed for a life of chastity, poverty and obedience, emerged. Their new gold wedding rings glistened in the sunlight, rosaries and bibles clutched to their bosoms, heavenly light shining in their eyes. A local photographer, determined to catch the 'rapture' of the moment, moved ahead of them with a rousing, 'Smile, Sisters, smile.' He was the first to meet his doom, slipping on the lubricious surface, and hurtling down the incline.

The new nuns, in their goodness and mercy, all ran to pick him up, to care for him, to give him succour, and all met the same fate. They skated this way and that, performing magical feats never before seen outside of Disney on Ice. Then, with what could only be described as a giant leap of faith, the grossly overweight Mother Superior launched herself forward to save her fledglings from their predicament, hoping to grasp them to her ample bosom and protect them from the waiting abyss. It was an ill-advised move. Misjudging the situation entirely, she slid on the top step and skied at full throttle into the group. They teetered momentarily at the top of the stairs, crossed themselves, then rolled over and over, black and white, black and white, black and white, down the steps, coming to rest on top of the hapless photographer.

Then all was still, all was quiet as the young nuns and their would-be saviour, the Mother Superior, lay on the footpath in a greasy pile, legs akimbo. Friends and relatives looked on in horror from the top step. At that point, I got on my bike and pedalled home as fast as I could. I didn't look back.

The evening news revealed that no one was seriously injured – just a few cuts and bruises – but police suspect it could be related to a series of anti-Catholic activities in the area of late. Possibly a serial Protestant. Oh brother. Now I'm some sort of fucking terrorist. And to top it off, that old drunk somehow managed to give police enough of a description for them to do an identikit picture of me. Not that it looks like me. Still. George and I will stay under the bed for the rest of the day.

Oh, Jack. If you were here this wouldn't be happening. Why did you leave me? Doesn't anyone have forgiveness in their hearts anymore? Where is my life going?

Sunday

Dad came and picked me up. I said I needed a change of scenery and could I stay for a couple of days. Truth is, I was worried that the police might be on to me. And I needed looking after. I needed some serious mothering. I am a lost soul.

Put George in a basket and brought him with me. Mum thought George was great. Took to him straightaway. George made himself pretty much at home and didn't spray once – well, only on the budgie when Mum wasn't looking. She decided it was time to clean the budgie's cage.

Mum asked me how Jack was and I burst into tears. Told her he'd gone back to Ireland. Mum said, 'Oh well, maybe next time, dear.'

Mum and Dad talked about the shocking incident at St Aloysius and how it could have been much worse, and what sort of a nutter would do something like that? I mean, a couple of nuns with bruises. It was hardly the Twin Towers, for god's sake.

Dad started to chuckle. He gave me a wink. Suggested the identikit picture reminded him of someone. Wonder if he guessed.

Lamb roast for lunch. Couldn't eat a thing. I am cast adrift. Rang Alison. Begged her to see me. She owed me one more session and I demanded that she honour our agreement. Decided to give her one last chance to put my life back together. After much deliberation, she agreed to see me tomorrow after school.

Monday

Not sure whether it was anything I said to Alison that triggered off the tragic events that followed in her office this afternoon. Maybe I should have been alerted to the delicacy of her situation when I arrived and saw her spinning round and round on her swivel chair singing, 'It's raining, it's pouring, the old man is snoring.' Her stripy hair was askew, eyebrows were still missing and scabs completely covered her upper lip. Decided to launch in anyway. It was time to tell her everything. If we were to get anything out of this final session, she would need to know the truth, the whole truth, the absolute truth, about everything that has been going on in my life. No point holding back now. I needed to find out exactly where I had gone wrong. None of this 'look it up in your diary' bullshit. I wanted answers and I wanted them right away.

Told her about the shag in the boiler room/member in the mouth misadventure with the Odd Job Man and my quest to undermine the Jamie/slut relationship using obscene phone calls, lipstick on the car, fish heads at the perfumery, resulting in the AVO and the cancellation of my invite to the barbie, then the crustaceans at the restaurant (but hadn't counted on the blue swimmer coming off the fork, which was how the slut broke her arm) and I thought Jamie would see the error of his ways but he didn't, so then the need to implement the creamy cake-licking plan which went awry with the rugby players saved only by Debbie Reynolds, just after the epiphany re Jack realising it wasn't just his cock I was interested in, but had in fact fallen in love, although I could see a problem down the track re the garbage, but there was always adult education, and all was rosy in the garden, but hadn't counted on the cat spraying the Collette Dinnigan and those two cunts sabotaging my life, hence the inevitable revenge with the oil on the steps, though the nuns took the fall, which was not really my fault, and now the police are looking for me.

'So you can see,' I said in my summing up, 'my life is totally fucked at the moment and I think it's up to you to put it back in place.' And then it happened.

Alison stood up. She looked at me with those blue, blue eyes. 'You know something, Margaret?' she announced. 'You were absolutely right. I – am – in – the – wrong – job!'

Then slowly, piece by piece, she began to remove her

clothing. I stared at her open-mouthed. First she took off her cardigan, then her skirt, then her blouse, her petticoat, her shoes and her stockings, carefully folding everything neatly as she went. It was almost as though some kind of symbolic shedding was happening. I begged for a bit of decorum in her behaviour, but it was clear that my presence was totally lost on her. She was caught up in her own little world.

The underwear was next. Her voluminous bra was unhinged and her giant breasts swung free as the breeze. I tried to escape but her substantial frame was blocking the doorway. She took her knickers off to reveal an astonishing Brazilian. I was totally lost for words. Finally, the comb she used to hold her hair in place was tossed away with gay abandon.

She stood before me like a giant pink Michelin man. I tried to point out how unseemly her behaviour was, I begged her to put her clothes back on. But she just threw back her head and laughed. She laughed and laughed, then ran out the door, down the corridor, past the other offices, out into the foyer, past the security guard and into the street, crying, 'Look at me, I am woman.' She then disappeared around a corner. I am guessing this will be our last session.

Heard on the late-breaking news that Alison had run the whole way to Luna Park and had a ride on the big dipper, the ghost train and the loop-the-loop before the police arrived and took her into custody. Felt really sad about it all.

Mum was watching the news too and asked me what might have sent a woman over the edge like that. I told her I had no idea. Which I don't.

Back in my own bed tonight. In my own little room

where I grew up. Nice big space under the bed, only no fluff to speak off. Can hear Mum ironing in the kitchen, Dad tinkering with something or other. I want to stay here forever. George is having a great time.

Lying in bed thinking of Jack. I really did love him. I'm sure we could have made it work. I miss him so. Only thing left in my life now is the panto. At least nothing much can go wrong with that.

Tuesday

At 10 am sharp, about fifty 'littlies' from the adjoining primary school were marched in and settled down for the panto. They were excited and a feeling of expectation filled the air. Their teachers were seated at the back along with those of our own staff who had a spare period. Miss McConnichy, Miss White the cookery teacher, Sue the phys ed teacher and Mr Daniels the vice principal were among those present. After a rollicking good opening – 'Here's the story of a selfish Princess' – the lights dimmed and the show got under way.

I suppose I should have stopped the performance immediately I realised there had been a major cast change. Amanda and Sheridan had taken over as the swineherd and princess. It was vanity, I suppose, and foolish pride, knowing that they were the only two who could carry off the main roles and make me look good in the eyes of the school. Had I known, in fact, that Amanda and Sheridan hoped to be expelled on this very day, to pursue their life ambitions of hanging around shopping malls, video parlours and going surfing, I could have prevented what followed. But all this is only clear in hindsight. Amanda and Sheridan would have their final revenge on me at last.

Ann gave me a quizzical look when Sheridan appeared on stage and introduced herself as Princess Margaret. I thought the name change was a homage to the departed, smoking English royal, never for a moment considering it to be a parody of myself. I was at a loss as to what to do, but as soon as she opened her mouth to sing, I was captivated along with the rest of the audience. Her rendition of 'Someday My Prince Will Come' was a triumph. The littlies thought she was hysterical, especially when she sent everyone off to the dungeons. Amanda also performed brilliantly as the swineherd. All was going swimmingly until the scene in the garden where the swineherd meets the princess for the first time.

PRINCESS: What are you doing in my garden? This is private. Can't you read the signs?

SWINEHERD: I'm sorry, but I'm blind.

(*Princess goes up to the sign.*)

PRINCESS: Here – this is what it says: P-R-I-V-A-T-E. Now you know. So go and wait somewhere else or I'll have you –

(*The swineherd turns around taking his cloak off to reveal himself as a handsome young man.*)

SWINEHERD: You'll have me what?

At this point there was some nervous shuffling from the staff at the back of the hall. It was clear that Amanda had stuffed something down the front of her tights.

PRINCESS: (*to audience*) He is very handsome, don't you think? But what is that down the front of his pants? What do you think, boys and girls?

The littlies, of course, got right into it. Suggestions ranged from 'I think it's a dickie' to 'Looks like my dad's penis' from one of the more mature students.

PRINCESS: Well let's see now, shall we?

The princess went over and put her hand down the front of the swineherd's pants and pulled out a pair of socks. The littlies thought it was hysterical, of course. Miss McConnichy was now trying to attract my attention as Sheridan waved the socks around in the air.

PRINCESS: Well, what a cheek. It's a pair of socks. You were trying to trick me. I'll have you boiled in oil.
SWINEHERD: Oh yes. I'd like that. The hotter the better.
PRINCESS: In that case I'll have you flogged.
SWINEHERD: You are soooo kinky. I'd like to be flogged.

Nervous laughter from staff.

SWINEHERD: So tell me about Princess Margaret, who lives in this castle. I've heard she's really mean and horrible.
PRINCESS: Oh no, she's sweet and warm and wonderful and nice.
SWINEHERD: I've heard lots about her. I heard she met a dwarf at a club and got warts on her private parts.
PRINCESS: Oh no, you've got it all wrong. It was an ingrown toenail.

Kids thought that was hilarious. Staff, however, were all very uncomfortable now. And I was certainly starting to worry.

SWINEHERD: Didn't she have a boyfriend called Jamie? Didn't he dump her to marry someone else?

PRINCESS: Absolutely not. The woman involved was a Lorelei. She lured him onto the rocks in the River Rhine. He didn't dump Princess Margaret at all.

At this point I was alerted and more than a tad alarmed. This material had a familiar ring to it.

SWINEHERD: I heard she lost her licence for drunk driving. That's why she rides her bicycle everywhere.

PRINCESS: She likes a glass or two. Helps her think more clearly.

There is something quite fascinating watching an accident about to happen. Part of you wants to stop it and part of you wants to see how much damage will be done.

SWINEHERD: Isn't she having an affair with the janitor at the local school, St Augustine's? Name of Jack?

PRINCESS: Of course not, that's just a rumour.

SWINEHERD: I heard she had sex with him in the boiler room at the school, then sucked him off in the garden shed.

At this point everyone on stage froze. The adults in the audience were now in a state of shock. I realised, of course, that all this was coming straight from my diary. Clearly those little sluts had read it. I had been outed. I knew it was time to stop the show. Miss McConnichy was already on her feet.

'I think that will be quite enough,' she cried.

The primary school children, who were obviously still

enjoying the panto, were suddenly hustled towards the door by their teachers. Confusion and outrage reigned. Miss McConnichy was trying to pacify the primary school staff. She had herself vetted the panto and this was obviously new material, she tried to explain. There would be a full investigation, she assured them.

After the primary school children had been herded out, Miss McConnichy turned on Amanda and Sheridan. What were they doing? What were they trying to achieve? In response A and S did this huge number, saying they knew all this stuff about me and were too scared to tell anyone, because they were worried that they wouldn't be believed, and felt that their morals along with the morals of the other girls at school were in jeopardy. Thought that if they exposed me in public by way of the panto, they might be protected from my wrath. They mentioned that I already had an AVO out against me and they were frightened of me. Those little cunts. They started crying and Miss McConnichy told them it would be all right. They were safe.

Miss McConnichy then turned on me. 'Is it true?' she said. 'Did you have sex with Jack in the boiler room?'

'And sucked him off in the garden shed,' yelled Amanda, still pretending to be upset and in shock. I looked around. All the staff who were in the hall were staring at me. Ms White the cookery teacher, Pamela from the art department, Sue the phys ed teacher . . . At this point I knew I was totally fucked. Right, that's it, I thought to myself: if I'm going down, I'm not going alone.

I turned on A and S. 'If you read my diary, you little arseholes,' I said, 'what about Halloween night?'

Amanda cried out, 'I told you we didn't do the vodka.'

'Didn't you read the bit about Miss McConnichy and my Aunt Penelope gnawing at each other's genitals in the very same boiler room? How come you never mentioned that?'

There was silence. All eyes turned to Miss McConnichy.

Miss McConnichy blanched, staggered a little and clutched at her heart.

'What?' came a little voice from the back of the room. It was Ms White the cookery teacher. 'What are you saying?' she said tightly.

'I said that my aunt was giving head to Miss McConnichy in the very same boiler room on All Saints' Day. "Keep going, Pen",' I cried. ' "To the left, yes, that's it . . . I'm coming, Oh yes . . . oh yes . . . oh yeeeeeeeesssss!" '

There was complete silence for a few moments. Then: 'You slut, Claire,' screamed Miss White the cookery teacher, who suddenly launched herself at Miss McConnichy. She wrestled her to the ground as we all stared in amazement.

'It was just one of those things, Mary,' cried Miss McConnichy. 'I couldn't help myself.'

I started laughing so hard I nearly wet myself. I left while the other staff were trying to pull them apart. I grabbed my belongings from my desk and cycled home.

The police were waiting out the front when I got there, asking questions about the church fiasco. Dana, of course, had pointed the finger. Guessed it was me from the identikit drawing. She was so pissed off at being dropped from the wedding party and me not lending her my spotty dress.

There was no point denying it.

Tuesday, four months later

Alison says I should start writing my diary again. 'Put everything down, everything that has happened,' she said. 'Get it all into perspective.' She thinks it might help. 'Writing a diary has certainly helped me,' she said. 'I feel like a new person. It's helped put my life back together. I can see clearly now where I went wrong and I am now able to face things again.'

She's not sure whether she wants to be a psychologist anymore. 'Maybe I'll try something else,' she said, 'like natural therapies or alternative medicine. Not sure whether I can hack listening to people's problems day in and day out.' We both had a good chuckle about that.

Alison's not a bad old stick when it comes down to it. She's going home tomorrow, so that will be a pity. The doctors feel that she's recovered now from her breakdown. I'll miss her. She said if she decides to start up her practice again, I'd be more than welcome. She's sure she could handle the challenge. Anyway, we're going to meet for coffee one day.

Sunningdale is quite nice for a loony bin. Although I like to think of it more as a rest home. Beautiful old Victorian buildings, lovely grounds, rolling lawns, a fish pond where you can sit and watch the carp for hours, nice staff, excellent food (athough Mum still insists on bringing in some 'good home cooking' in a thermos).

Another two months to go and I will have finished my time. Larry's lawyer friend appealed my sentence for the nun/church business and said I was mentally insane when the incident occurred, due to a build-up of personal tragedies in my life, the loss of Jamie, the loss of Jack, losing my licence, the pressure of my work. Jury was sympathetic. (Lawyer made sure it was stacked with Protestants who in fact found the event very funny.) The nuns forgave me, which is nice, although one of them saw it as a sign from God and ran off, never to return. The photographer was less forgiving. I had to undergo a psychiatric assessment and ended up here.

Much to my amazement, Alison was here too. She had a bit of a nasty turn when she saw me for the first time – the staff had to restrain her – but bit by bit we've become quite close. The hairs have grown back on her upper lip. I suggested she should sue the electrolysis people. It's supposed to be permanent, after all. She said she'd think about it.

'No, no,' I said, 'you need to be assertive.'

'You're right,' she said, 'I'll do it. And what about the pink streaks?' she asked.

I told her that grey definitely suits her better. Didn't mention the eyebrows, which never grew back. Nor the Brazilian. I didn't want to hurt her.

We sit out here in the sun, side by side, every day. It's amazing the people who rally around when you're in trouble. Sometimes the people you least expect – like the moron, for instance, Ned. He's been great. Aunt Penelope flew in from Paris to act as a referee (even after all the stuff I said about her). Ann and Larry have also been wonderful. They visit every opportunity they get. I consider them to be my very best friends.

My sister Harriet has been a tower of strength, and so

have Mum and Dad, of course. Mum is looking after George and he's become quite attached to her, which is just as well as the landlord gave me notice because of the cat and then had the cheek to put in a bill for the fence. (Dad went around to see him. Took some bottles of his vintage home brew. After a couple of glasses, the landlord forgot all about the missing palings and declared George was more than welcome to stay. Something quite magical about Dad's amber liquid.) In any case, I thought it best to give up the place. Need a fresh start. Will stay with Mum and Dad for a while when I get out of here.

No word from Dana. Heard on the grapevine that John dumped her and went back to his wife. I did try to warn her. Ha ha.

Amanda and Sheridan were not expelled after the panto, much to their angst. Their slag mothers had other ideas. They had visions of their beloved daughters finishing school and going on to university to become lawyers. They blackmailed the school into keeping them on. The library has now been finished. Miss McConnichy is at present on extended leave somewhere in Vanuatu.

Jamie and Lorelei went to Bali for their honeymoon and she came down with dengue fever and boils. I couldn't have been happier. What goes around comes around, so they say.

What now? An exciting future to look forward to. Alison says I should take time out to look at my life . . . look at maybe where I went wrong, what patterns I was repeating so that I can make some changes and move on. All the wonderful lessons to be learned. It's a whole new beginning, she says.

Lots of opportunities presenting themselves. Think Aunt Pen was right. I'm not really cut out for teaching. Not sure what I'll do. She wants me to go to Paris and stay with her for a while. Think this is a great idea.

Got a letter from Jack. He said he thinks of me often. Maybe I'll pay a visit to Ireland on the way. Who knows?

I think a lot about what happened. In retrospect, maybe I wasn't ready for a relationship, maybe I was on the rebound, and maybe I did use Jack. Next time it will be different. I will make sure I don't repeat destructive patterns. I will learn to accept people for what they are. I will try not to be a snob. I will try and keep my ego in check. I will learn once and for all that the world does not revolve around me, me, me.

Only one thing that worries me – do people ever really change?

Acknowledgements

Thanks to my agent Anthony Blair for his gentle prodding, his humour and his friendship; to Rose Creswell for her encouragement; to Jeanne Ryckmans and Renee Senogles for their enthusiasm and support; to Jo Jarrah for a great edit; to Darian Causby for his brilliant design; to the always friendly staff at the Cameron Creswell Agency; and, to the wonderful team at Random House.

A Year in the Merde
by **Stephen Clarke**
(Random House Australia)

There are lots of French people who are not at all hypocritical, inefficient, treacherous, intolerant, adulterous or incredibly sexy . . . They just didn't make it into my book.

Paul West, a young Englishman, arrives in Paris to start a new job – and finds out what the French are really like.

They do eat a lot of cheese, some of which smells like pigs' droppings. They don't wash their armpits with garlic soap. Going on strike really is the second national participation sport after pétanque. And, yes, they do use suppositories.

Stephen Clarke gives a laugh-out-loud account of the pleasures and perils of being a Brit in France. Less quaint than *A Year in Provence*, less chocolatey than *Chocolat*, *A Year in the Merde* will tell you how to get served by the grumpiest Parisian waiter; how to make amour – not war; how *not* to buy a house in the French countryside; and the perils of slippery dog poo (650 Parisians hospitalised per year).

'*A word-of-mouth must-have for le tout Paris.*' The Guardian

'*Clarke is able to distil, wittily and gently, the difference between Us and Them.*' The Sunday Times

The One That Got Away
by Lee Robert Schreiber
(Random House Australia)

A true story of what happened when one man contacted his old flame.

Have you ever Googled an ex? Ever wondered what happened to the first, the truest and/or the greatest love of your life? Have you ever considered how that person would respond if and when you did contact (let's say) her today? With dismissive laughter? A restraining order? Tears of joy?

Lee Robert Schreiber broke up with his girlfriend twenty-five years ago. He's not sure how encountering her after all this time will bring him closure, but he's tried everything else and nothing has come near to the depths of affection that he felt for this one young girl way back when. Pathetic or romantic? You make the call. Schreiber made the call (actually he emailed her).

This is his (and her) poignant, often hilarious and absolutely true story of the kind of love you never recover from.

Happy Days
by **Laurent Graff**
(Vintage Australia)

'It's not a long book, but it takes you far.' marie claire

What kind of man buys his grave at the age of eighteen and chooses to spend the rest of his life in a rest home at thirty-five? Meet Antoine, the curious hero of Laurent Graff's *Happy Days*, an odd young man who somewhat prematurely acquiesces to his terminal destiny.

The ultimate fatalist, Antoine decides to play hooky from life at the Happy Days Retirement Home. Despite the pronounced difference in age, the residents accept him, and he quickly settles into a routine as the life of the party, the sex toy of the nurses and the best friend of an Alzheimer's patient called Al. It's a carefree life until the arrival of a dying woman with whom Antoine forms a close bond and goes on a very special journey.

'Graff makes you question, laugh and melt.' Elle

'A slightly dark comedy that also works as a little philosophical tale.' Lire

'There is a little bit of Merlin in Graff, or Mary Poppins. This novel is supercalifragilistic.' marie france

Seeing George
by Cassandra Austin
(Knopf Australia)

A fairytale for adults about love, marriage and mortality

While filing away documents at work, Violet is interrupted by a new staff member, George. From the moment she sees him, Violet knows that George isn't ordinary. He surprises and enchants her in ways that her husband, Frank, never can.

In two years of marriage Violet has never kept anything from Frank, yet she can't bring herself to tell him about George. Simply describing her new friend leaves her speechless. But some secrets are impossible to contain . . .

Now, fifty years later, it's Frank's turn to surprise Violet – by asking her to stop seeing George. Why, having put up with him for so long, is Frank finally taking this stand? Does seeing George still have the power to end their marriage?

From a fresh, original voice comes *Seeing George* – an irresistible tale about truth, trust and the waywardness of the heart.

Swing Symphony
by Christopher Lawrence
(Knopf Australia)

One morning I realised that I was close to Jimmie Lunceford's fatal age, causing me to entertain a strange logic. If all the good swingers like Lunceford and Gershwin – or Mozart for that matter – tended to die early, and I was still alive, it followed that I was unable to swing.

Swing Symphony is a witty and affectionate celebration of eccentricity, orgasms and the challenge of being middle aged. Guided by his 'stride' piano-playing, 78 record collector friend, Booker, Christopher Lawrence's search for 'a new song' takes him to a medieval village in the south of France. The cast includes the reclusive American cartoonist R. Crumb; Pete, the world's foremost Zorro enthusiast; and the persuasive Nini, doyenne of the disproportionately large contingent of piano tuners.

By exploring an exciting time in popular music when Duke Ellington, Artie Shaw, Benny Goodman and others made Swing the Thing, Lawrence learns that 'in order to swing, one first had to be able to hang loose'. But most of all, he discovers the welcome intervention of unlikelihood that can happen when one stops for a while to see the show.